THE WARDROBE

THE WARDROBE

Daphne Glazer

for Doreen
with love
from Daphne.

FLAMBARD

Acknowledgements

'Dressing Up' and 'The Swimsuit' have previously been published
in *Dressing Up* (Iron Press). 'Knickers' and 'As the Shoe Fits'
have been broadcast on BBC Radio 4.

First published in the UK in 2004 by Flambard Press
Stable Cottage, East Fourstones, Hexham NE47 5DX

Typeset and cover design by Gainford Design Associates
Front-cover photograph by Justine Lester
Printed in England by Cromwell Press, Trowbridge, Wiltshire

A CIP catalogue record for this book
is available from the British Library

ISBN 1 873226 65 9

Copyright © Daphne Glazer 2004

Flambard Press wishes to thank Arts Council England
for its financial support.

ARTS COUNCIL ENGLAND

website: www.flambardpress.co.uk

For all the editors of small presses
who are keeping literature alive

Contents

The Bra

When somebody says, 'Can I ask you a favour?', you can be quite sure that you will have something irksome foisted on you.

Tina recalls the moment clearly. She was in the staff room at the end of afternoon school and Mike, looking haggard, turned his striped, humbug eyes pleadingly to her: 'Can I ask you a favour?'

If only she had said, 'No, I'm sorry, I can't.' But that was impossible. She knew as soon as he spoke that she couldn't escape.

Would she take his daughter, Katie, to town shopping for underclothes, bras and pants – he didn't feel he could. 'Of course,' she said, 'yes, yes, no problem.' Except there is a big problem: Katie.

Tina whips through piles of outfits in tense succession:
Black trouser suit on … off
Jeans and T shirt, black leather jacket on … off
Camel coat over sweatshirt and matching trousers on … off
Denim jacket and jeans on … off
Back to jeans, T-shirt, black leather jacket. She sweats with irritation, knowing that she must wear appropriate garments for this ordeal. At school, kids can be totally put off learning anything if you look old-fashioned, too conventional or fuddy-duddy. She remembers scorning Miss Winters, her maths teacher, because of her hideous woven bunion-pocketed shoes and her massive steel hairgrips, with the result that nowadays she is utterly defeated if she has to contend with percentages or fractions – the very sound of the words invokes terror in her.

1

Saturday morning and here she is having to take this child shopping. She could have been tidying up at home, marking, getting her schemes of work up to date, having a swim, going to the gym ... anyway, pleasing herself. Instead she must endure this difficult child. Had Katie been a sweet, chatty girl, things would have been quite different. How pleasant life was before the appearance of Katie.

The first time she ever saw Mike was in the staff room on an afternoon when Lawrence was declaiming his latest sonnet and the rest, faces twisted in annoyance, heads down, were trying to mark assignments. Mike looked across at her and winked and that hooked her. For her nothing is quite as attractive as a sense of humour.

From then on they have rarely been apart. Tina looks back with nostalgia on those after-school drinks; lazy sex-filled late nights; spontaneous meals out; cinema visits; weekends clubbing; country walks; swims.

When he told her he was divorced and that his twelve-year-old daughter lived with his ex-wife in Edinburgh, she thought: Well, not brilliant but at least she's several hundred miles away.

Only it hasn't turned out like that at all. No sooner did Mike ask her to move in with him, than Katie arrived on a visit.

'Come and have dinner with us,' Mike said, 'give you two a chance to get to know each other.'

Tina glares at herself in the hall mirror. February – freezing weather and the rain like grape seeds pelting the windows. She'll be frozen in this rig-out; get pneumonia; be off school; her classes will fail their GCSEs and A-Levels.

The dinner. Just thinking of it brings Tina out in a cold sweat. She has given up smoking but could almost restart at the memory of that occasion.

The scene: Indian restaurant.

Actors: One smallish but not microscopic, swarthy, rubber-faced forty-year-old man with excitable striped eyes. One distracted, nervous, reasonably attractive twenty-eight-year-old woman. One big, blank-faced, glum, monosyllabic twelve-year-old.

Action: twelve-year-old says, 'I don't like Indian food, Daddy.' Daddy orders chips and omelette for child. Child pulls a face and wrinkles up nose when grown-ups' chicken biriani and chicken rogan josh arrive. Child will not speak. Woman tries school questions. No answer. Never any answers.

What an evening! On arriving back at her own home woman needs stiff shot of brandy to recover.

After the dinner Katie returned to Edinburgh and things seemed back to normal, but then five days later, before Tina told Mike her answer about moving in with him, the bombshell: he announced that Katie was having problems.

'She can't hack it with Rob – that's her mother's new boyfriend – so she wants to stay with me.'

Ever since Katie's arrival Mike has been busy making arrangements for her schooling and new life. Of course they can't manage any more exciting interludes and life has been running according to a rigid timetable. Katie must be dropped at school, picked up, meals cooked etc.

As she drives over to Mike's, Tina listens to Classic FM on her car radio and tries to let herself float on a Mozart flute and horn concerto.

She rings and Mike comes to the door – she has the key of course but feels it wouldn't be tactful to use it.

'Why didn't you come in?' he looks surprised. She catches herself whispering, 'Better this way.' He still doesn't understand.

'Katie's just coming.'

It takes Katie a good half-hour to appear and Tina waits, shoulders braced, for her arrival, ears straining. When Katie does show up, she maintains the same blank expression and stands in the kitchen doorway without speaking.

'Oh, hi, Katie,' Tina hears herself burbling.

'All set are you, Katie?' Mike says and his voice sounds too loud and cheerful.

The child doesn't speak.

Going to be a bundle of laughs is this, Tina thinks.

As she drives into town with the silent girl beside her, she searches for some topic with which to open a conversation.

'How's the new school, Katie?'

Silence. Panic bubbles up in Tina. Her stomach clenches and churns. She fixes her eyes on the road. Two possibilities remain open to her: repeat the question; ignore the kid completely and pretend she hasn't put the question. When she has given up all hope of any response, the girl mutters, ''S all right.'

'Good.'

Well at least she can actually speak – now perhaps a conversation might develop.

'Have you any ideas what you might like to buy this morning?' Tina makes a big effort to charge her voice with energy and enthusiasm – she is with her doltish Year 11 group, trying to sell them Shakespeare, but they are dozing after late-night video watching and no breakfast.

Silence again. Rain splattering the windscreen, wipers scraping. The silence stretches tight between them and Tina twitches when the prim voice says, 'No.'

'Right, well, I suppose that makes it easier, doesn't it?' Oh talk to yourself, Tina grunts to an invisible person in her head. 'Your Dad said bra and pants.'

This could be a tactical error if for some reason the kid finds these objects difficult to discuss.

'Mummy normally buys my clothes.'

'Yes, I'm sure she does,' Tina tries to maintain an even tone and be matter of fact. She urges herself to keep going and steer clear of arguments. 'Well, perhaps now that you're older, this will give you a chance to decide for yourself.'

There is no response. With relief Tina accepts the card from the machine at the entrance to the car park. The arm jerks up and she drives in and parks the car. This is not going to be an easy morning

Tina perks up as the cloud of scents from the cosmetic counter hits her nostrils. They step onto the escalator and travel up to the first floor, and the mirrored wall throws back reflections of a peg-doll child and a harassed-looking woman, and for a second Tina wonders who they are.

The bras hang on fixtures, an array of underwired satin cups, scarlet, black, pale blue, maroon, blinding white lace scrolled with embroidery; Wonderbras plunging steeply to a pert bow or a seductive little rose. A special display announces 'Glamour Lingerie' and below it sprawls a bronze girl lounging on her side supported by one bent elbow. She is naked but for a white bra, the cups outlined in black jimpy bits and decorated with intricate embroidered flowers, and a microscopic pair of matching briefs. Her breasts pout languidly from the cups and her eyes carry a veiled seductiveness. Padded bras; balcony bras; bras to reduce the apparent contours of your boobs – all droop from fixtures or are displayed in discreet boxes from which a girl's face beams out. Her skin is always smooth and honey-coloured and she has no embarrassing bits bulging above or below the sides of the bra. Long shiny hair drips to her shoulders. You expect somehow to find her when you open the box, or at least to discover some magic conferred on the bra by the promise of her perfection – but no, the contents invariably disappoint in their ordinariness.

Tina stares at the cup sizes. They go from 32AA to 40C and beyond. She almost forgets the child in her scrutiny of the bras and is surprised to find her staring at the carpet.

'Well, plenty to choose from here, Katie,' she says in a hearty voice. The girl's lips twist in a small attempt at a smile. 'What size have you normally been having?' Perhaps she shouldn't have asked such a direct question. 'Do you want to have a look at the boxes and see if you can see anything similar to what you would normally have?'

As she turns over the boxes and stares at the pictures, Tina is in a moment with her mother in M&S when Tina must have been about twelve. First bra.

'You just need something simple – girls' ones.'

Only she didn't want something simple – the hideous white cotton, undramatic things that her mother was touching with such fondness. No, she wanted the sort she'd glimpsed in specialist lingerie shops made of slippery satin moulded to your shape so that when you wore a tight-fitting sweater you curved – not too much and not too little. She ached for scarlet or black and not cotton, not horrid floppy cotton, so utilitarian. Mandy Walters had a red bra and everybody envied her. When she wiggled into the classroom, you looked; you could make out the shadow of it inside her blouse and it emphasised her grown-upness. She wasn't some flat-chested kid, nor did she have boobs down to her knees. It was vital to be just the right size. If you weren't, the rest whispered about you – 'Just look at her!'

But of course it had been the white cotton and they travelled home on the bus with Tina in a deep sulk. On arriving back they found Grandma making tea.

'Just got Tina a bra,' her mother announced. Tina scowled with mortification.

'Is it a secret deceiver?' Grandma said and smiled.

'No,' Tina snorted, 'it won't deceive anybody, and it's pathetic.'

Katie doesn't appear to be making any headway. In fact she seems not at all interested in the boxes.

'Any joy?' Tina says.

'Not really.'

'Well what about the colour?'

On receiving no response Tina makes herself glance at the child's face and she sees a fat tear glistening on Katie's cheek. 'Oh dear, whatever is it?' She puts an arm round the girl's shoulders, wondering if she will be rebuffed, and tenses herself against a burst of prickliness. Much to her amazement, it doesn't happen.

'I don't know which.'

'I see.'

'I've never had one – at school it's awful in PE – I hate it. My Mum said I didn't need one – but I do – but …'

After further negotiations Katie withdraws to a cubicle with several boxes of white bras in different sizes. Tina stands waiting, her eyes rest unseeing on the women examining the display racks, whilst her head whirls with a sudden glimpse into the child's misery. The tear sparkling on the pale cheek returns her to a day long gone, the day her mother said: 'Your Dad's left us.'

The pain of loss stabs her somewhere in the solar plexus like the thrust of a blade – she hasn't expected a thing like this on a Saturday morning amongst bras and irritation. Embarrassingly she finds her own eyes pricking with tears.

By the time Katie emerges sometime later having decided on a 32B Tina is composed and smiling. Katie seems adamant that white is what she wants, and white flower-sprigged briefs.

Standing at the pay desk later with Katie beside her, Tina listens as Katie confesses how in her old school she was bullied and how she hated it and felt a freak and was too embarrassed to tell anybody.

'Let's have a snack in the café below, shall we?' Tina says.

As they descend the stairs Tina feels the coil of tension in her shoulders easing out and giggles with Katie as she describes the antics of her new hamster, Snuggles.

When they're sitting at a small table eating egg-mayonnaise and cress sandwiches and sipping tea, Katie actually smiles and says, 'Thank you for taking me shopping.' And Tina wants to hug her and tell her it will be all right, she will come through, but instead she grins back across the table and says, 'We'll have to have some more trips together.'

Down to the Foundations

Georgie is a rebel and always has been but she isn't the sort to launch herself into head-on confrontations. She prefers the subversive method, like saying yes but really meaning no and acting accordingly.

Considering herself avant-garde she visited the piercer when she was sixteen, and in his basement premises she reclined on a black plastic upholstered dentist-style chair that made her bottom sweat, whilst a spooky oldie in jeans, battledress top, cowboy boots and a thick gold earring drilled her belly button and fitted a stainless steel ring. The pain made her want to shriek but embarrassment saved her. The man assured her, 'You'll be back. Kids get a high out of this.' Of course she has not gone back since, though she never admits this to friends.

Piercing is a lot more painful than tattooing – well, she had her first tattoo done when she was fourteen, though the man thought she was seventeen. When her mother saw the blue and turquoise dragonfly perched on Georgie's upper arm, she looked appalled.

'You do realise it's there for life, don't you? It might go septic.'

Her mother invariably takes the pension-attitude to everything. The long-term view has never interested Georgie. In order to escape similar warnings and predictions, she did not mention the matter of the belly ring. Six months later when she happened to wear a tiny navel-exposing T-shirt, her mother spotted it.

'What on earth!' she said. 'No, you haven't. Whatever possessed you? You'll get blood-poisoning.'

By this time Georgie was able to present a nonchalant front and bluff it out.

This rebellious attitude caused her to sneak off into town with her mates when they were meant to be sitting in lessons discussing *Macbeth* or going through the causes of the Second World War, with the result that she extricated herself from school at sixteen without any qualifications.

Now three years later, after a series of strenuous jobs like 'cold calling' where enraged householders yelled down the phone at her that no, thank you they didn't want any fish and never to ring their number again, and a spell of night work in a care home, she is back in education. This time she is on an Access course.

Things on the Access course are rather cosy. Classes take place in an 1890s redbrick building where everything bumbles along in an idiosyncratic way, unlike the tense clattering regime in the main college. Most of the course members are mature students: women returners to education who have expended their early energies on bringing up children and now at thirty-five, partners having flown, want to start a new life; men squirming their way out of a chequered past, and others who have been made redundant from industry.

Amongst these men is Shaun of the shaven head, single earring and an eyebrow-ring that pincers his flesh, like a hook snagging in a fish's mouth. When he talks his conversation spurts out in excitable cigarette-perfumed gusts.

Georgie has been interested in Shaun from the very first moment she saw him. He is an older man, somebody with a scored face and knotty body – quite different from Mike, a boy of her own age. Mike's lankiness and the lack of lines on his face, his pale unblemished neck, all seem too young, too unmarked. Shaun carries the weight of other lives around with him.

The class (the men, that is, and Georgie and her friend Sall) tend to slope off to the pub on the street opposite after classes. This is a traditional watering hole and not of the new theme-pub variety, where meals are served and the interiors specialise in lots of Swiss-chalet-like, heavily varnished pine furniture. No, it has a resolutely unreconstructed appearance. Elderly men from the nearby estate crowd the bar and even more ancient ones sup their pints at tables obscured by twines of cigarette smoke. Drought-cheeked ladies bang away at the bandits, their faces puckered in avoidance of the smoke from their cigarettes.

Against this background, plans have been hatched for an end-of-term student fancy-dress evening. Georgie always sits beside Shaun who cracks jokes and tells her about his past life. He has been a model and a sailor who travelled all over the world; he has also slept rough on the streets of London and been a druggy and a beggar. In yet another life he has run a second-hand car business and subsequently a second-hand furniture shop; he has also dabbled in jewellery sales.

'Wow, you've just about done everything,' Georgie has told him, eyes shining.

'Well, now I've decided I must learn something – get a paper, you know, trouble is though, I can't seem to remember stuff,' and he guffawed.

On her way home from class Georgie generally sidles past a shop before which people rarely halt. Instead they quicken their pace and shoot by, eyes on a point well ahead. The window contains amazing things: models often in PVC minis, rubber knickers, crotchless briefs and bras with nipple holes. Most of the garments are either black or scarlet. A poster shouts: Blow-up Sheep available here.

After the date was announced for the end-of-term bash, Georgie was passing the shop window and noticed a bald-headed model strapped into a sexy black corselet. She decided she would breach the taboo of the intriguing place and go in, although at first she couldn't quite bring herself to do so. But then after she consulted Sall both girls entered the shop together.

Before pushing open the door Georgie glanced up and down the street, making sure they were not observed by anyone, but at that very moment a bus swayed by. She was sure all eyes must be riveted on them – in fact she tangled glances with a man on the top deck and blushed.

The assistant could have been selling lingerie in M&S and not crotchless briefs.

Oh yes, of course, she could try on the corselet, no problem.

Georgie imagined herself prancing about in the corselet, wearing black fishnet stockings and knee-high boots with dagger heels and a sliver of skirt, which grazed her knickers.

'So, what exactly will you be?' Sall wanted to know.

'Why a dominatrix of course,' Georgie said and hugged herself with glee.

'Oh right,' Sall said and made no further comment. She was to be Cinderella, in an old full-length Seventies dress belonging to her mother.

Georgie on this Friday evening up in her bedroom dressing for the occasion strikes up attitudes before her mirror. She is a study in black and scarlet. From time to time she brandishes a riding crop lent her by a horsy girl on the course. Absorbed in her antics, she doesn't realise that her mother is watching from the doorway.

'Georgie, for goodness sake, what's this?'

'Just my fancy dress – like it?'

'I don't know how you can bear to squeeze yourself into that iron lung. I've been put off corsets for life – when I was little your grandma used to send me to the launderette with her mother's corsets. They were massive pink things with laces and I was so embarrassed.'

'Mum, you've got it totally wrong – these aren't like that.'

'No, but I wouldn't like to wear that thing – it's like bound feet.'

12

'Don't suppose you would – anyway, it's got nothing to do with feet.' Georgie grimaces into the mirror and admires the way the corselet presents her breasts like two well-risen buns overflowing their cases. 'You've no need to go off on one – bound feet, for heaven's sake!'

'Do you know in Victorian times women used to have their lower ribs removed to give them a smaller waist?'

Georgie groans, 'Mum, you are so – so lacking in imagination – so uncool.' Her gaze flicks to her mother's elderly Levi's, sweatshirt and trainers. They aren't anything but mumsy and have no style, no image, no drama. She imagines whipping off her long coat to reveal her corselet in all its splendour.

By the time she and Sall arrive at the venue, which is in an old brick structure behind the main college tower block, they have reinforced themselves with two or three Malibu and cokes and twitter with excitement.

Someone whom she takes for Shaun is already there in a weird masked crowd at the bar. As Georgie strides across in her toppling stiletto-heeled boots, she feels all eyes fixed on her.

Shaun turns round and says, 'Oo, I need to feel your crop.'

Georgie stares at the black mask and the mad eyes jinking in the cutout holes, and feels unsure.

Drum and bass blast from decks as a chap in a pull-on woolly hat spins vinyl. Pirates, princes, queens, Robin Hoods, and movie stars grin and gyrate.

The air is laced with the sweet heady aroma of spliffs, and groups split off and drift into the nearby commonroom, where they flop down in armchairs and beam at one another.

Georgie is led off by Shaun into this room. 'I like you in that outfit,' he says, and the eyes behind the mask tadpole about. Never before has she noticed how pointed and sharp his little teeth look. He takes a long draw on his pint and the foam moustaches his mouth until he wipes the back of his hand across it. 'Do you know, you should always wear stuff like that – real kinky – yer, real kinky. When I lived with Hazel – oh Christ, she got to be a real pain – and the kids – she nagged, Christ did she nag. She wanted to own me. I didn't ask her to have all those kids, did I?'

He goes on recounting incidents, mentioning women's names, on and on.

Mike lopes over. He is Elvis Presley in splendid blue suede beetle-crushers and a white suit.

'Hiya, babe,' he says. Shaun gives him an evil look since he is still in mid-narration. Georgie is hemmed in by boredom, and the bones in the corselet press into her waist and belly. Shaun, now in real *Ancient Mariner* mode, shows no sign of ever stopping. 'And after that, will you believe it, she fucked off.'

People keep offering pints, which Shaun accepts, grinning and choking on his ever-present roll-up.

'What about a dance?' Georgie says.

'Na.' Shaun places his hand on her leg and the roughness pulls at the fishnet. Georgie bridles with irritation. 'Got a pint here.'

'Yes but …'

'Later, later – what's the point?'

His hand roves higher, causing little pulls all the way up the stockings, then he reaches her bare flesh and the suspenders. 'That's what I like,' he says, 'girls in suspenders and stockings, oh yer, you can't beat little stunners in suspender belts and stockings.' His teeth chomp the air and he takes another glug of beer.

Georgie feels herself shrinking and almost losing her identity as Shaun bulges over with talk and his life unfolds like some huge MFI furniture construction kit, which can't be assembled because the instructions are missing.

'I'll go and find Sall,' Georgie mutters. She doesn't like the way Shaun has begun to eye Mike.

She finds Sall in the buffet crunching down handfuls of salted peanuts and stuffing herself with sausage rolls and gossiping with some of the older women.

'Hi,' Georgie says and pretends she's enjoying herself, biting into a chicken vol-au-vent. Several ham sandwiches later, she feels she will burst. The corselet holds her stomach in a vice and constricts her breathing, and the cups cut into her breasts.

Shaun lurches in. 'Oh, there you are, sweetheart, love of my life.' He drapes himself about her. His face has taken on a deep burgundy glow and his eyes gleam through the mask slits. She gasps for air.

'What's up, sugar?'

Sugar. She can't bear it, people don't call each other such things, it is seriously uncool and so boring.

'Nothing,' she says, 'I'm just off in there,' she says indicating the drum and bass room.

'Why? Don't you wannabe with …'

'I want to dance.'

She totters off, feeling shivers down her spine.

After picking out Mike's blue suede shoes, she clops over and begins to gyrate next to him.

She hasn't been there long before a figure bulldozes through the capering couples. He heads straight up to Mike and tries to fist him in the face. Mike jumps back and crashes into someone else. 'Sorry, sorry,' he says, 'I think Shaun's off his head.'

Shaun prepares for another go at Mike. Georgie feels if she has to spend another moment in the corselet she will scream, and without another word she rushes out to the cloakroom, grabs her coat, and once in the street flags down a passing taxi.

No sooner has she reached her bedroom, than she unhooks herself from the corselet and hurls it to the other side of the room. Next, she unzips the boots, hauls them off, shrugs on her bald cotton dressing gown with the elephant on the pocket, and pads downstairs to make herself a mug of cocoa.

She sits in a beat-up armchair in the kitchen, quaffing her cocoa and luxuriating in the feel of her unfettered flesh, whilst she mentally goes through a list of experiences never to be tried again:

1) piercing
2) older men
3) corselets.

And she wonders if the last two do not have something in common.

It is time, she thinks, for something new and challenging, but she hasn't yet decided what this might be.

Knickers

The revelation came to Jayne in the swimming-bath changing room: knickers are the indicator of a person's sex life.

She was stripping off absentmindedly with most of her attention fixed on what the kids were doing, when she noticed Emma, her eldest, peering at someone. Immediately she gaped too.

The woman wasn't young, must be in her forties and she sat drying her feet. All of her shone like oiled teak. On her shoulder an intricate tattoo flowered. She had biggish breasts with dark-brown nipples that she seemed in no hurry to hide, but what was really arresting were her knickers. Could you have called them knickers? When she rose to stretch into a shirt and pull on some baggy Indian cotton pants, it was obvious that they were merely a thong, which passed between the cheeks of her bottom. Her front was covered by a little pouch.

Nothing about the woman, however, was as unsettling as the thong. It suggested all manner of sexual fantasies. A woman's knickers also gave you ideas about her partner, perhaps her husband; though a woman like that couldn't possibly have a husband. She would have a partner, perhaps partners ... the partner would have sleek black hair in a ponytail and wear a black or pale linen suit and be an actor or someone in Arts Management. A big calf bag would be slung over his shoulder.

Two teenage girls were with her and they seemed ordinary enough. Their mother looked the type of woman who would have gone on the trail of an Indian guru and worn beady exotic things and danced with dervishes had she been born fifteen years earlier.

All the way home from the baths, Jayne pondered on the thong. Then she became aware of the lemon-coloured sky and the hectic twittering of birds and she felt distracted. Later, when the children were in bed, she considered the contents of her underwear drawer, which comprised a pile of off-white, fawn or pink cotton briefs; the sort she bought in packets for the same amount you might expend on a single pair of more elaborate ones. They were all saggy and undistinguished, a bit girly perhaps, certainly not the sort of gear you would wear for a close encounter.

The idea of a close encounter had been nudging her for months, but now it was urgent. She felt sixteen again, even fifteen, and she was waiting for something to happen, but there was the danger that it might not. For the rest of her life she might stay becalmed on this sandbank, i.e. in the semi where she had moved with Gary when they got married. But at thirty-three and three kids later and Gary departed with his twenty-one-year-old secretary, whose underwear would be some minuscule black silk number for sure, her options had dwindled. What she might feel herself to be inside did not correspond to what those on the outside saw. Men's eyes, she supposed, simply whisked over her: she was a mother of three, no longer a single entity and furthermore she was battered at the edges.

The knicker-drawer scrutiny did not arise by chance. No, something else precipitated it, something which started out as exciting but which was fast becoming a nightmare: the blind date.

Chrissy, a smart twenty-six-year-old in the office where Jayne worked, had initiated it.

'You need to get out,' she'd said. 'There's more pebbles on the beach – in fact there's this Darren that Andy knows.'

Talk moved onto a foursome, but then for some reason Chrissy and Andy couldn't make it.

Jayne was to meet this Darren at the entrance to the railway station the following day.

After last night's gazing into the abyss of the knicker drawer, she took the decision to spend her lunch hour whizzing round the shops in search of some fitting underwear. But what would be fitting? Thirty-three wasn't old, although suddenly it felt like it.

In M&S the escalator whisked her up to the first floor where tanned female torsos modelled blindingly white underwired bras and satin briefs with high legs exposing acres of thigh. Exquisite girls in slithery French knickers frolicked on posters. Knickers of every kind imaginable prinked on fixtures and counters: lace and nylon, black, deep-blue, maroon, white, eau de nil, all slippery smooth, some decorated with microscopic bows; some flocked like embossed wallpaper. Then there were French knickers with wide flappy legs, the sort you imagine 1920s ladies wearing as they reclined on sofas and drew on cigarettes in long tortoiseshell holders.

Jayne hovered by them, touching, imagining. There were stout packs of pink and blue flowered briefs; Daniel Lamberts that would practically reach your armpits occupied their own fixture.

The French knickers looked slinky, beguiling, but you couldn't possibly wear those under anything really figure-hugging, because they would leave a massive ridge and, anyway, they would be monumentally draughty in winter and the crotch might ride up between your legs.

High-cut briefs would slide into the crack in your bottom and have you forever trying to ease them free.

She lingered, fingering some sly black satin briefs. Black. She was thirteen, out with her mother shopping for underwear.

'No, you don't want black at your age, it'll make people think things – red? No way. Look, get those nice flowered ones – cotton, that's what you want. Nylon makes you sweat.'

Black, sweaty nylon knickers … yum! She scowled at her

mother, who never seemed to have been young. She was yearning for something sexy and sophisticated.

Looking up, she caught sight of a person in the mirrored pillar before her. Who was that frowning, nondescript type in the navy-blue jacket and pleated skirt? She averted her gaze with shock and started fumbling through the virgin-white cotton knickers. Very young girls in swimming-bath changing rooms wore those. She hesitated. Crisp white cotton would appear ultra-clean; give a hint of newness – but as a mother of three kids she was hardly new. The paradox of the matter was that having been married since she was eighteen and never really having got to know any other man like she knew Gary, she felt a complete novice in the games of men and women.

With Gary there had been all that time at school with hand-holding and snogging at night in the road outside the house and then some daring attempts by Gary to unfasten her bra or fumble into her flower-sprigged briefs. That was what you had done at fourteen – all gradually over a period of weeks, months, years. All very obsessive.

Whilst she examined the white briefs, she wondered what new rules there were and then she stopped short.

Here she was, dwelling on the expectation of a sweet seduction, whereas such a thing might not happen at all. Having been married all those years made her assume that being with a man must lead on to sex as a natural progression. Her cheeks began to tingle with heat. It must be something to do with the weird weather …

Gary had walked out six months ago. For weeks she cried herself to sleep but the routine of breakfasts, dinner money, school runs had forced her to keep going.

First there had been rage: the brute had betrayed her, ruined her life. Next came despair, she was abandoned. Following on that she wrestled with his reason for leaving – she wasn't attractive enough; it was her fault he had left, because it all came down to faults. She had always been one of those people who at school when anything went missing or any crime was committed imagined herself to be the culprit. Now, today, the past seemed worn out, something new was disturbing her, excitement made the air zing.

The lunch hour was practically over. She'd have a terrific rush to get back to work in time. She grabbed up some French knickers, black with a flock design on them.

By the time she was grilling two vegeburgers, because Emma and Rachel were vegetarians, and waiting for Paul's chicken burger to cook in the oven, she was wishing she had decided not to go.

She could, of course, fail to turn up, but if she did that, Chrissy would find out and she would never hear the last of it. There was no escape.

'What's that in the bag?' Emma spluttered through a mouthful of burger.

'Oh nothing.'

'But it's got to be something.'

'Just leave it alone, it's only some pants.'

'Let's have a look.'

'No, no, just get on with your food.' She sweated with embarrassment.

Before the babysitter arrived, she tried on four outfits, examined her stretch marks and broken veins and the flab round her waist and twisted backwards to take in the full impact of her cellulite. This was worse than preparing for a school exam or a driving-test. A sick feeling gnawed away at the pit of her stomach. She did not resemble the torsos in M&S or the poster girls. She had also lied to the kids, they thought she was off out with Chrissy.

Darren would be wearing a rosebud in his buttonhole. That

sounded romantic and even more calculated to increase her panic. She was not going to sweep up in a long floaty dress or a mini exposing endless legs in sheer black nylon. One last time she glowered at the neat conventional figure in the navy blazer, white blouse and long pleated skirt.

She travelled into town by bus and, with her heart banging, she trotted round the corner from the bus stop and came up facing the entrance to the railway station. He was there. She had a brief view of a big chap in a navy suit with a rose in his buttonhole. He looked very stiff and formal.

'Oh hi,' she said, 'you've got to be Darren.'

'That's right.'

She couldn't think what on earth had made her do this.

'Right, er well,' he cleared his throat, 'shall we find a nice quiet pub?'

'Er yes …' She panicked, casting round for something to say. That book, the bestseller in the States, told women to find out men's interests, ask loads of questions about their jobs, keep them talking. On the other hand, if you wired into the job scene too fast, the man might think you only cared about financial considerations. You were instructed also to be inaccessible, keep them guessing, a veritable Scheherazade, yarning away. She saw herself muffled in veils elocuting whilst the potentate reclined on his day bed leering at her ankles.

After some more hesitation he launched her into the hotel bar at the railway station. Jayne sank down into a deep chesterfield and waited, studying his back as he stood at the bar.

His ears stuck out a bit and he shouldn't have had his hair shaved so high, it gave his neck and head a scraped parsnip look. When she had been a teenager, her mother had said: 'Be careful; they're only after one thing.' All men were monsters and rapists. Then along came Gary and men's dangerousness receded. Now after years of cosiness it had re-emerged, but somehow changed, sharpened: men were wolves after all in sheep's clothing.

'Oh, that's better,' he said, taking a good swallow at his pint. She nipped at her half of lager and scrabbled in her head for a topic of conversation.

'Been quite warm for this time of year,' he said, before she could start in. 'Yes … must be the hole in the ozone layer.'

They managed a half-minute on that, about another half on pollution generally and the way everything seemed to be going to the dogs. Meanwhile an Oasis number yowled in and out of the crumbling Health Service and the chaos in schools. This led on to stories of sons' and daughters' progress at school. Jayne unearthed the fact that he'd got two sons, eight and five, who were with his divorced wife, Anne.

'Anne left me,' he said.

Did she commiserate, say, Oh dear, I'm sorry, or mutter indelicate words about his wife? She left it at 'Oh dear'.

'You get over it.' He took another long swig. Four halves of lager or so later, she explained about Gary. He said he missed his kids. They compared the toy boys and girls of their respective ex's and smiled at each other.

'You know,' he confided, 'it all makes you start wondering what you did wrong, doesn't it?'

'Yes,' she said.

'I was real worried about meeting you,' he said.

Actually his ears looked quite friendly and the parsnippy shape of his head was oddly comforting. 'Ditto,' she said. She admitted that she hadn't known what to wear. He said in his lunch hour he'd wandered about buying himself some more casual gear but then didn't wear it in the end.

She found herself imagining him gazing at those discreet white cartons of boxer shorts and trying to decide on the pattern, tartan or stripes, or maybe fingering the Y-fronts, or even the daring abbreviated numbers.

They left at eleven p.m. and made for the taxi rank. Jayne felt they were survivors of a shipwreck, and when he reached out and took her hand, she glowed with its warm firmness. Getting into the taxi she glimpsed the sky and it hung like a pair of enormous navy-blue star-spangled knickers and suddenly she knew it was spring.

A Vested Interest

'Is it a big one then?' How big is big? Jenny asks herself. A pity she let slip to Doreen at work that her birthday was looming. And now here it is: the Big One – and she would like to forget it but her son and daughter won't let her and have invited her to a celebration dinner.

She takes furtive nebs at herself in the sheet of mirror by the escalator as it reels itself up to Ladies' Fashions on the first floor and her face wattles back at her – a stodgy, suety individual who needs brightening up. This Saturday morning she has spent an age rattling coat hangers in her wardrobe as she inspected rows of discreet pleated skirts, sensible pastel blouses, and dresses and jackets in caramel or beige man-made fibre – all she supposes very staid and toned down. She has always been a brown person. Well, working at Thompson's Timber Merchants for years – in fact ever since Bernard left her for the other woman – has encouraged her in this. Mr Edward, the boss, liked everything to stay the same. To have tried a different colour scheme might have upset him, but perhaps she is only making excuses, she has to admit that she has always put most of her energies into being a mother.

Anyway, she is a twin-set and perm sort of person, someone who likes to know where she stands and never gets out of control. A very efficient typist according to Mr Edward – but Mr Edward has now sold the firm to a young thrusting individual with a mobile phone and a huge black BMW. He shot in last week, took the office in at a blink, pursed his lips and, giving a little grin, said: 'Hm, have to make a few changes around here

– needs updating to the twenty-first century, I think.' Then he strode off.

Doreen said, 'Crikey, I think he means us, I bet he'll get rid of us. Only a matter of time and it'll be computers and bimbos in here.'

Bernard, her ex, Jenny reflects, is really an older version of the new dynamic boss. When he married her, he liked her because she didn't contradict him – well, she can't bear big rows. Her own parents never stopped bickering with each other. But after a while she simply didn't fit with his image of the successful property developer. He's on his number three wife Jody now, who isn't much older than Jenny's daughter, Donna. Of course Peter and Donna have always kept up with their father and things have remained on a civilised basis.

She is in a curious mood this morning. It is as though she has jogged along safely for years in the same way, but suddenly everything has shifted and even Donna swivelled a critical eye at her the other day and said, 'Mum don't you ever think of trying another colour?'

On reaching the first floor, she is attracted by brilliant colours in a boutique. She sees mad pink and orange tops and, oh yes, a violet one the colour of her favourite pansies and then a sparkly, silver creation like frosty pavements. She lets the silky texture thrill her finger pads and imagines herself wearing such garments, but with what? No absolutely not, she could not possibly be seen in something so daring, anyway these tops are pared down, diminutive, figure-moulding garments and they would show the dimpled flesh at the tops of her arms. She feels discouraged and is about to turn away when a perky voice says, 'Can I help you?'

Jenny looks into the face of a slick young woman in a hot pink top and tight-fitting black trousers, who balances on mules that highlight her maroon toenails.

'I was looking for a top and something to wear with it.'

'A vest was it?' the assistant says, patting the clothes in a familiar way, somehow confirming their seductiveness.

A vest – so these were vests!

Vests: the word conjures up Liberty Bodices, Vick and stuffy noses, itchy armpits, curd-coloured hairy stuff poking out from collars, ridges left by short sleeves under long-sleeved shirts, excuses in changing rooms and furtive manoeuvrings.

Mother laid down: Never cast a clout until May's out. On blistering May days when other girls skipped out in the school's blue and white check summer frocks, she was condemned to wear her vest, shirt, cardigan and skirt. 'Just because there's a bit of sunshine don't go flinging everything off or you'll catch a chill.' Chills hung in the air, waiting to pounce and confine you to bed with a chest that bubbled and piped.

Yes, vests were what was concealed but never successfully enough. Somehow people always knew that beneath even the most alluring upper garment, this other hideous skin lurked. Vests were a state of mind that signified unathletic, weak-chested, nervy creatures, lacking all zing and sex appeal. Other girls slinked to the shops to buy sweets in T-shirts or revealing blouses, which set off their pert shapes, no matter the weather. And there she was, bosomless, front flattened to a board, muffled in thick vest, jumper and coat of course.

'Yes, a vest,' she hears her voice say with enthusiasm, 'I'd like to try several please.'

But what has she done! The assistant shows Jenny into a cubicle where she faces a merciless sheet of mirror. The searching orange light focuses on her crow's-feet and the nervous corrugations of her forehead. She eases off her blouse surreptitiously and dodges her reflection.

First she struggles into the violet vest. Horrors. She is confronted by her wilting arms the colour of dead chicken flesh and her bra straps slipping through the spaghetti straps of the vest. Impossible – never. She blushes at herself. One garment (she remembers hearing Donna referring to something similar as a 'boob tube') becomes a boa constrictor and swallows her, and she must fight her way out of it panting and emerges with hair tousled like a mop head. She just manages to extricate herself, thank God, before the assistant's head peeps round the curtain.

'Any luck?'

'No, afraid not, it's … my arms you see.'

'What you need is a little bolero if you want to cover them, that would go well with some black trousers – I'll find you some in a tick.'

The girl returns holding a silver vest with its own tiny jacket and some wide-legged slinky black trousers. Jenny regards them dubiously. She has begun to feel very deflated. 'Well, I expect I can give them a try – thanks very much.'

With amazement she discovers that the trousers hug her hips and don't accentuate the droop of her backside and the silky silver vest when worn plus bolero looks rather stunning – in fact she is surprised at the sight of herself. All she needs now are some spiky stiletto-heeled shoes.

Donna zooms up to the house at eight. 'Ready Mum?' she calls from the hall and her eyes open wide with surprise. 'Wow, that looks good!'

The accolade. Off they drive. 'Where are you taking me then?' Jenny asks, looking at the faces of her son and daughter.

'It's a surprise, wait and see.'

They draw up before the Civic Hall and Jenny is puzzled – after all this isn't the usual place for a dinner invitation.

Jenny follows Donna in and they are shown upstairs to a room with a bar which is full of people and above them a silver and scarlet banner shouts, 'Happy 50th birthday, Jenny'.

A buffet has been laid out in one corner and a DJ messes with electrical equipment on a stage.

'Goodness,' Jenny squeaks, staring at the people who have all turned to gaze at her. Panic makes the colour whoosh up her chest and she is glad of the tiny vest, which prevents her from steaming. Fifty, for heaven's sake, they didn't have to know that. She feels overwhelmed and Donna must have noticed because she says, 'I bet you're wondering how we got everybody here, Mum?'

'Well, I am rather.'

'Your address book. I just went through it.' Donna is triumphant. How could her daughter have done this? Little does she know the ramifications of it all. Jenny tries to seem pleased and murmurs, 'How very clever of you, Donna, what a brilliant idea!'

They have begun to sing, 'Happy birthday to you, happy birthday dear Jenny!' A burst of clapping follows. Champagne corks leap and Donna hands Jenny a frothing glass. Jenny takes several long swallows and the fizz prickles in her nostrils.

In the crowd, some of whom she doesn't recognise, she spots Bernard, her ex, and his Mark 3 wife, Jody, and she clops over in her strappy stilettos. Bernard, now raspberry-jowled, has started to barrel slightly. With men it's always the middle that goes first. She thinks of her chicken-flesh arms; thank goodness their monstrousness is hidden.

'Lovely to see you both,' she starts, taking another deep swig of champagne.

'Yes, good to see you, Jen,' Bernard drawls, eyeing her up, 'nice outfit.'

They are quite matey these days.

Jody, after greeting Jenny, has turned to Jenny's son, Peter, and his friend and they seem to be locked in animated conversation.

The DJ has finally mastered his electrical wiring and a burst of music booms forth. Nobody moves, so he wheedles into the microphone, 'Come on birthday girl – gents and ladies, where are you, let's celebrate.'

The 'Birdie Song' lollops along and Jenny is urged forward by Donna and Jody into a giggling circle. Bernard won't be drawn in. Peter and his mate position themselves beside Jody. Soon they are flapping their elbows, shaking their backsides and doing the actions at the wrong time, giggling fit to bust and gasping with hysteria. After they have stuck out their hands into the middle, they are off again.

Whilst they pause waiting for the DJ's next record, Jenny sees Doreen. They hug each other. 'This is a grand do,' Doreen pronounces, 'happy birthday, love.' They indulge in some savage shoptalk and begin to plan a strategy for outwitting the thrusting new boss.

Jenny hasn't danced for years, not since the Bernard times, and she is wafted into euphoria and flings her arms about and shimmies her pelvis in a rock'n'roll number. She bumps about opposite a tall balding chap, someone with a satin voice and battered mobile face, who keeps singing the words and whom she doesn't recognise. When the music stops, he says, 'Bet you don't remember me, do you?'

'No,' Jenny says, 'I can't say as I do.'

'I'm Geoff Everson – we were at school together, remember? Ran into each other ten years since.'

'Goodness,' she says, 'yes – right – well when I really look at you.' She has a vague memory of exchanging addresses. Geoff of course was one of the bad boys. Though she does remember him putting up a TV aerial for her. She discovers his TV business has expanded considerably and he is now doing digital satellite aerials. She can just see him, an ageing James Dean, swarming on rooftops, clinging to chimney pots, outlined against the sky. Quite heroic in fact.

They have another bop and then it's time for the buffet and everybody hawks down on the dishes of samosas, exotic beany things, cubes of chicken tikka, rice salad and various platters of rosy ham and barbecued chicken legs.

For once Jenny is no longer on the periphery of things, eyes alert for disaster, making sure that everything is under control – now she swims along, basking in the rollicking movement of laughter and voices and hands touching her arm. She lets the creamy smoothness of a shrimp vol-au-vent lie on her tongue and takes a deep draught of white wine and sighs with pleasure.

Then comes the cake, a big white iced square decorated with silver flowers, icing curlicues and mauve violets with yellow centres. 'Speech, speech!' they bellow.

Jenny, who has never spoken publicly in her life, grins round at them all, her family, Doreen, the bad lad Geoff, old school friends and says, 'This is just so lovely – thank you Donna and Peter and thank you all – it's magic.' She breaks off fearing she might cry.

More music. Off she capers. They are all on together now bopping up and down. The room is hot and the beat sizzles. 'Let's twist again.' She giggles and zizzies down, bending her knees and flings off her bolero, which Geoff catches and drapes over his shoulder. As her shoulders and elbows wiggle and her backside shakes, she feels gloriously free and manages to creak up again before falling about laughing. Geoff pirouettes with her bolero. Somebody lets off party poppers and they fly about, winding them all together in a pink and blue mesh.

Tableaux float across Jenny's vision: Jody pressed in a clinch with Peter's mate; Bernard with cricked back and knees trying to come upright after the twist; Doreen bent double with the giggles.

And then it's over and they move into a big circle, arms round one another and someone says, 'Three cheers for Jenny.

Hip hip hooray!' and bad boy Geoff squeezes her waist and it is then she realises he has still got her bolero festooning his neck.

'Do you mind?' she says and nudges him, retrieving her bolero.

'Well I just thought if I nicked it, it'ud give me an excuse to phone you,' he says grinning and gazing with appreciation at her three-and-a-half-inch rapier-heeled silver shoes, 'anyway I like your shoes.'

'Oh well, in that case ...' Jenny says, grinning back.

The Gamblers

Audrey enters competitions in the same way that some people fill in lottery coupons, and that is how she came to win the spring cruise on the luxury liner and to meet Irvine Waller. It is also the reason for her fluttery night. Audrey's fluttery nights are ones where she flips alert, straining to listen for robbers creepy-creeping along the landing to strangle her. The panic this time is generated by her forthcoming day at the races with Irvine.

She has been awake since before six. It can't be the same here on dry land, she worries, the magic will have evaporated. The cruise was special. Besides, worst of all, she might be found out.

Once she has made herself a pot of tea and jammed two slices of bread into the toaster, her insides begin to settle. Staring at the asphalted back yard (she calls it the patio) and the wheelie bins, which she has tried to disguise beneath the forsythia's trailing tendrils, she allows herself a few minutes to dally in the memories of burning blue skies and porpoises leaping from glossy seas; sun loungers on decks occupied by kapok-haired, wattle-jawed ladies with honking expensive voices sipping tequila slammers and G&Ts; bands playing and lengthy dinners served by waiters in white uniforms, squeaking to and fro on plimsoled feet.

Best though were the haunting tropical nights with the liner throbbing like a giant heart and the moon, a strange gold fruit, suffusing the black waves with phosphorescence. She was up on deck, standing at the rail on the first evening, when someone hahhemmed behind her and she turned to find this tallish chap in evening dress which lent him a raffish air. When he was younger, he must have been blond; now his white hair lay close to his skull and had a tarnished tinge like an old smoker's moustache.

'Nice to get a breath of air. Hope I'm not interrupting your reverie?'

She remembers muttering something, which he obviously interpreted as encouragement.

'Name's Waller, Irvine,' he said. 'Your first cruise?'

'Oh no.' She tried to give the impression of being laid-back, a world traveller. At all cost she must not reveal her humble origins or that she could never under normal circumstances come on a cruise such as this – well, be on any cruise for that matter – even the ones on the ferry across to Belgium or Holland. All the people on the cruise liner were loaded. The women's freckled claws were blotched with diamonds the size of Disprins and the men had the vaguely complacent air of those who are so used to being in command that they do not look for insults. They were sharp enough underneath, though, she was sure of that.

At this point she panicked, expecting him to administer a questionnaire on foreign travel and catch her out, but she needn't have worried. He got launched instead on his own foreign trips: jaunts to India and descriptions of ancient temples, holy men, huge castrated men in diaphanous sarees wandering on beaches; the hum and craziness of Bombay, a world of wild traffic – motor rickshaws, scooters and bullock carts all going full tilt. He delivered this in posh, nasalised accents.

Sipping her tea and scrunching her buttered toast, she lets herself linger over that initial encounter with him. He has the sort of noble profile and bearing that she associates with suede loafers, cashmere overcoats and exclusive men's clubs with servants waiting on the members. She imagines him living in an expensive London flat in a Georgian terrace in, say, Russell Square, with a little ornate metal balcony rail. The brass doorbells on such houses always gleam. He'll drive a Jag with leather seats and a walnut dashboard.

As he talked on that evening at the rail with his forearm leaning alongside hers and his dizzy blue eyes gazing into her face, he exuded a powerful aura of the affluent, the exotic and faintly decadent, combined with an aroma of smoked cigars and musky aftershave. This had the effect of empowering her to enlarge on a cruise to Egypt (which of course she had never experienced) and a visit to the tombs of the Pharaohs (at school Audrey had always been good at English). She was assisted in this by the fact that her best friend, Beryl, had recently described in great detail a package tour and the ensuing diarrhoea attack – of course Audrey drew a veil over this aspect of the trip.

In the following days she lounged by the pool, frequented the casino, where she watched Irvine languidly sliding counters about, and after dinner glided with him across the neck-breaking parquet as the band brassed up. She was swept along in a delicious dream.

During this time they exchanged life stories. Audrey tried to remain as mysterious as possible. He knows she has been made redundant but he doesn't know precisely from whose employ. She will keep it dark that she has worked for years as a manageress of a snack bar in Frazer's. She has led him to believe that she was private secretary to a very eminent man – in fact, she can almost see this man – someone not unlike Irvine, only of a more regular type, not quite as unusual. She isn't sure exactly why she considers him unusual but she certainly hasn't met anyone like him before. Irvine, she has discovered, is divorced, though he is very reticent about personal matters.

Anyway, she must get ready for the big day. He wanted to

fetch her from her house, drive over, he said, a mere sixty miles. Oh no, she said, he'd never find it, better she meet him in town. She couldn't possibly have him driving up to her terrace. The thought makes her blush. Nothing must disturb this fine romance for which she has always yearned. Men have shot in and out of her life like people through supermarket checkouts. There was that nice Eddie, but he had a mother who didn't intend that any woman should supplant her in Eddie's affection. Audrey nearly married Alan, a strong silent type – only with him still waters did not run deep and he could get very nasty and was tight with money. Terry always liked to have another string to his bow and Charlie preferred boys when it came to the crunch.

Horrified at the way time is passing, Audrey clops upstairs and into her bedroom where she has laid out her pale lemon suit, white blouse with ruffled neck and wide-brimmed lemon hat decorated with a bow of satin ribbon. This exquisite hat does not belong to Audrey – she has loaned it from Claire's Hat Hire shop.

When Irvine first rang and suggested the races, she almost declined because she knew from looking at pictures of Ascot on telly that women wore hats for such events and she couldn't afford one – well, not a proper hat – one of those elegant, eye-stopping creations beloved of society women. But because she was amazed at him actually phoning her, she said yes. Then she remembered seeing the hat-hire place in town. Claire, the proprietress, wore gold mules and flue-brush eyelashes and displayed the hats with the tips of crimson nails, touching them so lightly that you got an inkling of their preciousness.

Audrey tried on turbans and cloche hats, curly conch shells and velvet chamber pots, and finally the lemon one which of course had already been booked by someone else for a wedding – mother of the bride, Claire said – but if Audrey returned the hat the very next day, she might hire it – however she must make sure to have it back on time.

'Oh yes,' Audrey assured her, 'back on the dot.'

So now, she immerses herself in the dressing ritual. A day like this calls for the best of everything. She basks in the pleasure of new gossamer-fragile tights, a pure white satin lace-trimmed slip with matching knickers and uplift bra. She has had her hair coloured more of a honey-blonde than usual – and really, when she surveys herself in her dressing-table mirror, she can imagine that she did work for a Mr Graham Henshaw as his private secretary. Her boss will resemble those urbane suited gentlemen she used to see slipping into the snack bar regularly for coffee and a sandwich.

Audrey stands waiting before the First World War memorial where soldiers like bears swarm up a rock. They used to be clutching bayonets but these are long gone.

She stares at the soldiers from time to time and then takes peeks at her watch. People keep glancing across at her because of her hat. You wouldn't be wearing a hat like this unless you were off to a very important occasion. She recalls the conversation with Claire: 'My hats have even been to Buckingham Palace and taken tea at the Queen's garden parties; they've been at weddings, inaugurations, you name it – my hats bestow class on the wearers.'

The pearl-grey Jag slides to a halt, hovering on the road like a great moth. She is impressed by the springing jaguar emblem and would have liked to run her fingers over it.

Irvine is wearing a navy-blue and red spotted bow tie and a navy pinstripe suit. The heavy gold signet ring on the little finger of his left hand makes her want to swoon. She has a thing about men with signet rings on their little fingers, but the rings must be of a certain sort with substantial shanks and perhaps the face of the ring could be a seal. Here everything is perfect.

What shall she do with her hat? She can't really sit wearing it in the car because it might interfere with the driver. With care she swivels round and places it on the back seat.

'You look stunning, Audrey, I have to say so, utterly stunning my dear – and what a hat!'

Audrey feels her cheeks growing hot. This is all so right – the car is just how she has imagined it would be also.

'Did you have a problem finding me?'

'Oh no,' he turns to smile at her, 'a slight hitch with speed checks en route – the boys in blue, nothing significant.' He dismisses whatever it is with a wave of his left hand.

Irvine invariably talks in this way, and Audrey can never be quite sure what is happening. Things remain in a delicate haze rather like a Monet landscape. In one way she appreciates this in him. She has never liked the stark humpiness of everyday things.

The car scarcely appears to be moving as it sleeks along through the countryside.

'It seems so strange to be on dry land now,' she tells him.

'Yes, good fun wasn't it.'

She supposes he must travel a lot, and he nods and hints at various business trips, which are always cropping up.

Almost before she registers it, Irvine has parked the car and they are making for the entrance to the racecourse. The air vibrates with French perfume and body sprays from the knots of scarlet-lipped behatted girls and women in wafty pastels and imposing headgear. The men, lassoed with binoculars, hawk in on the groups and keep them moving. Audrey begins to get the notion, that such events are not purely social, and that beneath them skitter stomach-griping tensions.

Irvine seems very preoccupied once they have reached the enclosure and spends a lot of time with his head in a programme, periodically disappearing only to return several minutes later with a slight flush on his pale cheeks. Audrey is content to stare about her at the racegoers and then across at the racetrack.

It is quite a shock once the horses erupt onto the turf. She sees a line of creatures come zooming out of the traps, microscopic riders clinging to their backs like ticks as they surge by. Hooves drum, the crowd yells, the line sweeps round the track. All that can be seen of the riders are helmets, bright shirts, numbers and tight bottoms thrust in the air.

One race follows another. People scream and rage; betting slips are torn to shreds and tossed to the ground. Bookies windmill their arms in semaphore. Irvine displays little emotion at the outcome of each race and Audrey doesn't know whether or not he has been backing something and out of delicacy refrains from asking. She gets him to put a fiver on Arabian Knight, which trundles in last.

During a break in the proceedings Irvine steers her to a bar, which sells sweating pasties, sausage rolls and evil-looking beef sandwiches (sure to give you salmonella). There is also a buffet and Audrey scrutinises this with an eagle eye – after all she hasn't spent years in catering for nothing. Of course she mustn't comment, because private secretaries will not know one end of a vol-au-vent from the other.

'Enjoying it?' he asks.

'Well it's different,' she says, still smarting at the loss of her fiver. 'I get the feeling you could lose a lot of money here.'

'Without doubt,' he says and gives a sardonic smile.

A huddle of men argue in loud voices and a young woman displaying a lot of bosom sits at a nearby table in conversation with an elderly man whose eyes are clamped to her cleavage.

Audrey lays her hat on an unoccupied seat beside them – the trouble with such splendid hats, she realises, is that you can't wear them indoors.

'I do hope this isn't boring you?' Irvine says and gives her a deep swimmy blue look.

'Oh, not in the least – it's all fascinating.' Audrey sips a glass of hock and nibbles a smoked salmon sandwich whilst beaming at Irvine.

She has just managed to guide Irvine onto more personal topics and is congratulating herself on this, when a huge florid chap hoves up at their table. 'I say – er hope it's all right if I join you?' Without more ado he flops down on the lemon hat, and continues talking, quite unaware of the wreckage beneath him.

'Er …' Audrey tries, 'would you excuse me but …'

'Certainly. What a day!' the man howls, 'what a day!'

Audrey can scarcely sit still and stares at the man's mouth pulling into words but she doesn't take in what he's saying. At some point she hears him whine, 'Wiped out, totally wiped out.' Irvine nods sympathetically.

'Please,' Audrey tries again, 'please, please, you've sat on my hat.'

'Hat!' The man looks surprised and lumbers up, catching the table with his knee and upending his pint glass. Beer froths over the hat and the chair and dribbles onto the floor as the glass crashes down. 'Oh, sorry, sorry about this.'

Audrey takes the battered lemon object from his hand. She is almost in tears.

'Oh dear,' Irvine says, 'bad luck.'

The man, who is clearly drunk, burbles on about his losses. When it becomes obvious that he has no intention of leaving, Irvine glances across at Audrey and says that perhaps they should be moving on.

Once away from the bar Audrey can't help herself. 'It's ruined,' she says, 'just ruined.' Irvine looks bemused. 'It isn't even mine.' The hire story comes out. Audrey no longer cares. This, she thinks, is the story of her life, and when Irvine suggests that, well, perhaps they should call it a day and go, she nods in agreement, struggling to hold back her tears. If she were to cry, she would cause her mascara to run and her face would look like the Sahara after a freak rainstorm brought on by Global Warming. She can't imagine how she will face Claire, the hat-shop madam – and what about the mother of the bride?

'Perhaps it could clean up a bit,' Irvine suggests.

'No way,' Audrey says, remembering the scarlet nails caressing the hats, 'she'll know every dimple in the fabric like she knows the lines on her own face.'

They slither into the Jaguar and Audrey scowls out at the day, too upset to bother about the frown lines she is encouraging on her forehead and at the bridge of her nose.

The Jaguar hums along the road but Audrey takes no notice of the flashing countryside, and so jerks upright in shock when the car shrieks to a halt, having embedded itself in the back of a stationary vehicle.

'Damnation!' Irvine bellows, striking the steering wheel with the palms of his hands, 'damnation!'

He slumps against the wheel and only stirs himself when an enraged scarlet face bobs before the window.

'Didn't you see there's been an accident, man – a lorry's shed its load up ahead – for God's sake …' The man rants on about his car, his bumper, a wing knocked out of alignment etc. Irvine keeps nodding. Addresses have to be exchanged. The Jag's broken headlights gape like the staved in windows of a derelict house, or rotting teeth.

A long while later they resume their journey. 'This is going to take some explaining away,' Irvine muses.

'How do you mean?' Audrey says. She has been shocked out of her own misery by this new development.

'Oh, the car – well, you er see,' giving her a sideways glance, 'it's a hire car.'

'Yes,' Audrey says, understanding the problem intimately,

'that is a problem.'

'And you see, I haven't had a good day on the gee-gees.'

'Right.' Audrey finds herself smiling. In fact they both smile at each other. 'Well perhaps you'd like to come back for a cup of tea to drown our sorrows?'

'Sounds a good idea,' he says.

As the car swoops along, still purring after its little escapade, Audrey feels an exhilarating sense of freedom and bursts into inane giggles.

Fevers

The little transparent packages containing plastic sacks always plop through the letter slot about the same time. Straight after Christmas the first package arrives: Help the Aged. On the list of requirements are 'unwanted gifts'. Finding an outlet just like that for chipped mugs, shrill scarves or gasp-inducing toiletries proves very satisfying. Though I admit to certain misgivings and I try to wriggle out of my doubts: perhaps the mug isn't really imperfect; perhaps the scarf doesn't appear hideous to everyone. But what if I am not giving in the proper spirit? Wrestling with guilt, I climb the stairs preparatory to a search of my drawers and wardrobe. I ought to donate something of value; something which will raise money for the cause … The Aged. I ponder on the word 'aged' – 'aged' sounds far older than 'old'. In German there is a word *steinalt* – old as stone – *steinalt*, aged. I am prickled by the thought of shrivelled forms in food-splodged, flappy clothing, crouching in chilly rooms.

The wardrobe door swings open. I gaze at the navy suit, the velvet tops, the brocade waistcoat, the jeans, the gracious skirts. No, I can't donate those, after all I use them, don't I? A padded shirt skulks in the corner. I have scarcely worn it – that would be a good donation. I fold it and lay it in the sack. Nothing else. Progress to drawers. Slack, crotch-seeking knickers, prickly 32A bras, fuzzy tights, only one place for such – the wheelie bin.

The second drawer down provides a little worn navy sweater. Third drawer. I ease it full open and something catches my eye. Gauzy blue, purple, turquoise weave together. I drag out the garment and toss it onto the bed. Must be ten years since I've worn it. The colours have paled, though there is still an aura of opulence. Excitement sizzles around it. I hold it up to my nose and sniff, imagining that I can still smell the scent of those days and nights. It sticks in my nostrils, a warm, aromatic fragrance and it mingles with the dark pungency of male sweat and the scouring odour of antiseptics and disinfectants. I stand motionless with the shirt pressed to my cheeks.

Ward 14 is all that remains of the old fever hospital, a low building containing half a dozen cubicles. Mine faces a patio where you can sit out on wooden benches and gaze away over lawns shaved close as a crew cut and as furry.

Mazy roads weave around the lawns. Local ambulances bump along them from time to time conveying patients from the X-ray station or further afield. Squirrels shin up groups of silver birches and scrabble in flowerbeds amongst the roses. The scent from the flowers wafts sweet and heavy to me as I sit out waiting for something to happen.

Long stagnant stretches sag between the hypodermic needles probing arms, stabbing to find blood, and the weighing, the X-rays, the puffing and blowing into Peak Flow meters.

Mary groans that she must have a smoke and scuffles off to take a quick drag in the toilets where the nurse won't see her, because smoking is prohibited in the hospital.

Alex, a grey-skinned, oldish man, sits near me. He fixes on the drive below us. I know he wants to see his wife come slinky-bottom-wiggling up there but that doesn't happen often. His wife is a lot younger and very pretty. Her shoulder-length blond hair ripples about her face. Pink-cheeked, plump-lipped, you can tell that mouth kisses a lot and the sway of the hips and the poising of her stilettos make you think SEX – SEX in capital letters. Before her arrival, he fidgets and grows manic. Once she flutters down beside him, he stares at her maroon-varnished toenails and sulks. I hear him snapping and pleading and I strain to follow the dialogue but can't.

In this blazing summer weather the ground cracks, leaving deep fissures in the lawns and the grass turns brown.

Sun glances off the glassed-in corridors and it is like being in a conservatory. Some patients retire to lie on their beds in the long hot afternoons. Cleaners in yellow uniforms whip about on squishy soles, working Blue Jay cloths over sputum pots, lockers, bed frames, tubes, heart monitors, metal kidney bowls, in a constant dusting and swabbing. The floors exhale the searching pungency of disinfectant and it swells in the heat and tickles the nostrils.

After a time outside on the benches I feel suddenly tired and I go in and lie on my bed, lulled by the heat and the cut-offness of the place. Exotic plants thrive in such temperatures: pouting spotted orchids, passion flowers, short-lived, tropical blooms. This is the realm of dreams and hallucinations.

In a half-doze, drugged and relaxed, I see a face behind the glass, gazing in at me. The figure is tall and thin. Not someone you could ever call good-looking – shaven-headed, gristly cheek-boned – but the eyes send out hypnotic messages. I am stirred by this examination and terror rustles along the edges of my arousal. I close my eyes and refuse to look any longer. An auxiliary nurse pushes a tea trolley in.

'Tea, Debbie?' she says, 'Milk and sugar?'

The figure behind the glass has gone. I sip my tea, enjoying its blandness, and stare out at the hard blueness of the sky, which seems higher now that the day is turning towards evening.

Later a nurse rings a bell for dinner. Alex and Mary and two middle-aged women head for the recreation room and I join them. That's when I see the man who watched me earlier on.

'Now then, can we all get sat down?' the auxiliary nurse, Tracey, says.

'I don't really feel hungry,' Mary moans, 'I can't manage much.'
'Just have a try, Mary,' Tracey wheedles.

We are all here for tests, all waiting for something. It can put you off your food, but I feel ravenous.

'Debbie, this is Craig,' Tracey says, indicating that Craig should sit opposite me at the table, 'he came in this afternoon.'

'Hi,' I say, oddly disconcerted. The eyes look at me again and a strange charge zigzags between us. He nods. I dodge his eyes and turn to the ham salad and chips in front of me.

'He says I'm going down first thing tomorrow. Ugh, I can't eat this.' Mary pushes the plate away.

I don't mean to look, but my eyes rove over his hands as he slides up peas with the side of his fork or jabs at chips. The fingers are long and thin. A navy-blue snake writhes up his right arm. My eyes stray higher, over his black T-shirt to his throat and the pale flesh of his face, the beard forming a gun-metal shadow down the sides of his cheeks, a tattooed beauty spot high on his right cheek bone.

He watches me. The curved flaps of his nostrils widen; in their mobility they suggest tropical places, an exotic ancestry. The charge that leaps from him to me makes me so aware of his every move I can scarcely sit at the table.

I keep my head down and try to concentrate on the ham salad and chips. The others talk operations or make jokes. Old Doug, who has just taken his place, kids the women.

'Are we slipping out down to the Gun and Duck tonight then, Betty?'

'Just listen to him!' Betty snorts.

'We shan't be as chirpy this time next week,' Mary mutters.

'Oh, come on, lass, it's being so cheerful as ...' Douglas says.

'Keeps me going,' Betty grins at Doug.

'What was you two getting up to last night?' Tracey pauses beside Doug as she collects the plates.

Dinner over, I wander down the corridor by the cubicles and out. It is still warm. I know he has followed me and I can feel his force-field drawing me in. I want to run away but can't. I am held there.

'Nice night,' he says.

'Mm.'

'Getting visitors?'

'No,' I say, 'not tonight. What about you?' I watch his mouth. The sculptured curve of his nostrils is repeated in his lips that are quite thick I study the planes of his cheeks and shadowy hair follicles. A white scar traces his cheekbone. That beauty spot is scary. He has not answered my question but stares at me as though he wants something of me. The tension tightens.

'Are you from round here then?'

I tell him I live thirty miles away. He says he's from the town, no problem.

We sit down on the bench. Alex's wife has just arrived. We watch them going into his cubicle. Alex looks grim.

I shiver with the zigzags of energy springing off Craig. He tells of moving about a lot; factory work here and there; clubbing, being crazy about making music in clubs; his mother walking into the sea and drowning; an estranged partner – lots of things scattered about. I give him my broken three-year marriage, finding Jake with his lover, all that. Then it is lungs. In Ward 14 lungs are on our minds. Breathing. Breathing is life – where breath doesn't exist, life doesn't either. Breathing is the sea ebbing and flowing; susurrating, rasping, puttering, puffing. On the wards at night I hear those sounds competing. There are also night sweats, tightness; freezing times with ice compacted into your bones.

In my thin gauzy shirt goose pimples rise on my skin and I hug my arms about my breasts.

'They said a shadow, like.'

'Oh yes,' I say, 'a shadow.' I picture the shadow, a dense, grey shape blocking out the mysterious tracery of his bronchioles and air sacs so that they are filled-in patches of nothingness. A shadow.

He coughs. I listen to the dull, hollow sound. His eyes rake the filmy layers of my shirt, which hints at curves, almost reveals but doesn't. In it I become powerful.

We hear a bell ring. Visitors leave in dribbles. The first to clack away down the drive is Alex's wife. Well people don't belong here, and she can't escape fast enough.

Craig and I sit in the recreation room. The TV burbles away but we aren't watching. Betty and her friend and Doug lounge in easy chairs, patting banter back and forth.

The nurse's trolley squeaks down the corridor. Medication time. The shift is changing. We hang on, not wanting to part. A huge moon watches from the inky sky and splatters the lawns with phosphorescence. I want unimaginable things. My skin burns.

He talks of drum and bass and his fingers spider out a rhythm on the chair arm, but all the time he looks at me and we know something else is on our minds. This is a place where you must speak the truth: it is an on-the-edge experience.

A nurse hovers and so we have to separate. His cubicle is next to mine, separated by a window, but a full length flowered curtain prevents us seeing each other.

I slip into my nightshirt and lie on my bed, aware of him beyond that thin glass divide. From time to time I hear a hollow cough. The long whispery night has set in and moonlight pours through the small window above the door and drenches the floor in silver. Owls moo. Coughs splinter the silence and sometimes a buzzer goes and then nurses' shoes squeak on floor tiles and a voice babies someone. The late-night smell of brewing tea and making toast stirs my appetite. I sleep finally but am still caught in this magic trap.

Another day of the gauzy blouse.

We spend hours together, talking, laughing, looking. I study his face trying to interpret what I see there. The beauty spot hints at something dangerous. The wild side keeps him moving. 'I'm a rover,' he says and laughs. I watch his mouth. We are so near, our forearms almost touch and the down on my skin rises.

Earlier a white mist covered the silver birches and hung above the lawns and now the sun glances down and there is no wind. They take Mary out on a stretcher to the waiting ambulance. The ward seethes with expectation. More tests – blood tests, X-rays, physiotherapists.

'Don't go away, you two,' the nurse says, 'I need to know where you are if doctor needs you.'

We exchange glances and grin.

Another trolley is trundled out to the waiting ambulance by jocular men in white uniforms. Alex is on his way.

They come for Craig to see the doctor and I feel jittery. It is as though I have no past and no future: I am this me who belongs here with Craig and his shadow-damaged lung, and raging Alex and Mary who is terrified of operations, and Doug and Betty who flirt endlessly, and Tracey who tells us what she does with her boyfriend when she gets home.

In here you have strange dreams of golden moons and faces behind glass and paper-thin blossoms with giant phalluses at their centres, of being held and stroked, of touching flesh, of being kissed with open lips …

Half an hour later he returns, grinning. 'Next week,' he says, 'they'll do it next week.'

I can smell his skin and I stare at the navy-blue beauty spot, his dark stubble hair. The moment lasts for years, maybe forever. All the hairs prickle on my arms. The centres of his eyes grow huge. We sit side by side and don't speak.

He has his operation before mine and reaches the Low

Dependency Ward in the new main building first. My bed is wheeled in on a blistering afternoon. All the time in between the operation and now is a vague, pain-filled gap. My mouth feels dry and I long for water. My attention is seized by staring eyes. Craig understands what I want and he slides off his bed and staggers across, fills the glass on my locker from the water jug and holds it to my lips.

I am tethered to the bed by tubes and drains and can't move much. He touches my hand for the first time and all the nerves tingle. 'Oo,' I say.

'I've missed you,' he says.

On the day Craig is to be discharged from hospital, I am out of bed and able to shuffle about. My parents have come over to see me. The afternoon is heavy and minute black flies dart to and fro, thunder groans but no rain falls. Light-headed I try to concentrate on their news, but I can't stop replaying the sickeningly exciting jolt that struck between my legs and sent spirals of pleasure into my solar plexus and up my arms when earlier Craig placed his hand on my thigh as we sat outside sunning. We cannot leave each other alone.

Just as I am waving off my parents, I notice a blond woman arriving. She is quite tall, all boobs and legs and very casual in shorts and a scoop-necked vest.

'Could you tell me please where Ward 7 is?'

I direct her, but somehow I know she has come for Craig. I follow her down the corridor. She crosses to him.

Later as he leaves with her, I pretend not to be watching, but when they reach the door, he turns and my eyes meet his and I read the same hot longing there as before, and then he's gone.

I drop the shirt into the Help the Aged bag, take the bag downstairs and deposit it before the front door. On impulse I go out into the back garden. Late January and yet it is extraordinary mild. A lemon sky throws the pear tree and the horsechestnut trees encircling the allotments at the bottom of the garden into strong relief. The bright green slivers of shooting bulbs poke up from the borders. Dead leaves clot the patio. Hearing a craking, I look up and see a V of wild geese winging by, necks stretched out, wings flapping. The earth is rich fruitcake; pears have rotted into straw-coloured mush on the weedy lawn. I catch the wild white scent of viburnum. Butter-yellow jasmine peeks from a barbed-wire twirl of rose stems. I stoop to examine a ladybird half-hidden in a heap of damp leaves. Life is starting again. I can trace the pressure of it in the new green growths, a lightness in the air. Suddenly everything is possible. That is when I rush back into the house. Perhaps already the Help the Aged van will have collected the bag from the doorstep. I can't part with the shirt; I must have it.

The bag is still there. I draw a deep breath, open it and remove the shirt, weak with relief.

Secrets

'She was strangled with a pair of tights.'

'The intruder wore a stocking mask.'

Stockings and tights: dangerous killer weapons but also symbols of the subversive and exotic.

Great Aunt Dora worked in a bookshop in Charing Cross Road (not the famous one) and her flat was filled with all manner of expensive objects – ivory statuettes, jade bowls, a Lalique box and Persian rugs. She wore ivory combs in her hair and white pin-tucked blouses with a cameo brooch at the neck.

Edith can remember visiting her once as a child and being shocked by the strangeness and beauty of everything. Occasionally Great Aunt Dora came up North to see them all. She never married but that didn't mean she looked like Miss Webster at school. No, there was just something very daring about her. The last time Edith ever saw Aunt Dora was when a low-slung shiny black car zoomed up the road where cars never came and stopped outside their terrace, alerting everybody round about. The driver, who wore a long, belted coat and gauntlet gloves, leapt out of the car in one swift movement, strode round to the passenger side and opened the door.

The picture of Great Aunt Dora stepping out of the car is trapped in a cameo. There she goes, her skirt ripples over her thighs and her shiny ankles are exposed. Edith sees oyster-coloured silk stockings, smooth as whipped cream, and she imagines how they would shock your fingertips.

In that moment Edith vowed that when she grew up she would be rich and wear silk stockings, not horrid dark-brown lisle ones like Miss Webster's.

Edith's mother snorted when Edith told her about the silk stockings. 'I'd like to know what she did to get them.' Edith didn't know what she meant and her mother wouldn't say any more.

When Great Aunt Dora died, Edith forgot about her mysterious aunt for some years – anyway she was caught up in the drama of her own life: falling in love, catapulting into a wartime marriage with John, a boy who'd been in her class at school and who was a fitter in a sweet factory.

They'd been married two months when John received his call-up papers and was spirited off to France.

Edith moped for several weeks but excitement tensed the air; everything rushed at her in a new way. She might be alive one minute, dead the next. A piece of masonry might crush her to pulp out in the street or as she lay in bed at night. If she didn't live now, she never would.

Her best friend, Betty, suggested a night out dancing. There wouldn't be any harm in it. So it was gravy browning on their legs to create an alluring tan shade and an eyebrow-pencilled line down the middle of the calves for the seams. She dabbed Californian Poppy behind her ears and in the hollow of her throat, and wearing her favourite plum-coloured dress she clacked along in her sling-backs to catch the tram with Betty.

The band played 'Over the Rainbow' and tunes that could make you cry but there were also brassy, jazzy numbers where you swayed and wiggled, and it was during one of these that the American airman approached her. He was big and his teeth flashed when he smiled and he moved in a lazy powerful way. She was entranced by his foreignness and his mouth shaping words that didn't sound like English. He danced close. So close she knew she was doing wrong – but she wanted to go on and on and never stop.

And that was how it started – only nobody knew about the airman – not a soul except Betty and of course she wouldn't breathe a word and she never did – though in the end even Betty didn't know the whole story.

The airman gave Edith nylons, nylons that she had only heard about but never seen before. She adored their filminess and the shine they lent her legs. Standing before her dressing-table mirror, she admired how her legs curved and shone, and she remembered Great Aunt Dora's silken ankles and her mother's voice: 'I'd like to know what she did to get them.' She was locked into something scandalous, loved it and couldn't hold back even if it meant ruin.

By the time John got a sudden home-leave Edith knew she might be two weeks pregnant. Nobody will ever discover the truth about that though.

Edith's airman must be a very old man now, living some-where in New York City. John says his daughter, Maggie, takes after him. Edith dared not wear her nylons after John was demobbed, and she hid them wrapped in tissue-paper at the back of her knicker drawer, because somebody might have asked that awful question were she to have worn them.

Even Edith's daughter, Maggie, has been caught up in the romance of nylons, and like her mother before her she fell early under the spell of stockings.

She was probably fourteen at the time and travelling to school on the other side of the city and she had to change trams in the city centre. As she waited at the tram stop, she saw galleon trams rocking up Commercial Street and crashing to a halt. Transfixed she watched a coal-black tram driver spring down from his cab and walk off with his arm round the waist of a candy-floss-haired conductress who wore nylons with black seams and heels and black butterflies winging up the ankles. Her pale shiny legs and hair shocked against his darkness. He loped along with his great shoulders thrown back, swaying from the pelvis. She fell against him and they laughed together and it was as though magic particles radiated from the couple, sealing them off from the passers-by who gawped in amazement and muttered things.

All through lessons Maggie dreamed of the dusky driver and the blond conductress and the black butterflies flapping up shiny legs, and she remembered the sexy, audacious aura and she wanted something wild and colourful to enter her life and cut her free of boring lessons and homework.

Away from home at Teacher Training College, Maggie met a Nigerian prince and ran off with him to Lagos. Of course you didn't wear stockings out there, but by this time the potency of those shiny nylons with their black butterflies had done its work.

Lagos was humid, crammed with raucous life and scary. It seemed easy to die out there. The surf at Bar Beach looked idyllic, pounding on the white sand, but the strong currents could bear you away in a flash and a businessman staying at the Federal Palace Hotel had his head snapped off by a shark. People died of mysterious illnesses which were all subsumed under the general heading 'rheumatic pains'. Wandering one day at six o'clock sunset in the Lagos cemetery where bats dive-bombed over the breadfruit trees, she came upon the gravestones of early missionaries who had, it seemed, landed in Lagos in the 1870s only to die two weeks later of 'the country-sickness'.

The rains came drumming in thick rods on the corrugated iron roofs; the open drains overflowed. In the dry season the sun hung in a margarine ball directly overhead. Tempers snagged. Armpits sweated and itched. The frangipani gave off a scent that was so sweet it vibrated in Maggie's head. Homesick, she received letters from Barry, a married lecturer at the college where she had studied.

My Darling Maggie,
I miss you endlessly – come home! I am sending you
the fare. I had no idea how devastating this separa-
tion from you would be. I've left Mona and the
divorce is pending ...

Maggie eloped again, this time back to England, and as the
DC 10 lifted out of the humming bush, she breathed a sigh of
relief.

Now in her sixties, and still married to Barry, Maggie wears
trousers or jeans and ankle socks: she has given up on stockings
and tights – they are too dangerous. (Her past remains her
secret, together with memories of those black butterflies.)

The same cannot be said of Maggie's daughter, Emma, who
is a researcher and has grown up with tights so they are merely
objects of apparel, which she regards as commonplace. She wears
thin black tights and loafers and skirts that show off her peerless
legs; silver tights at Christmas, glitter on her face and hair, and
minuscule silver tops; stripy fun tights; jungle-patterned tights;
sexy fishnet tights. She has been a free agent, tried them all.

Being quite a tough cookie Emma has sailed through *affaires*
with aplomb. She believes in having fun.

Then, all of a sudden, things change. In the Senior Common
Room one Monday afternoon, she happens to look up from an
armchair where she is ensconced, to meet the concentrated,
sardonic gaze of a bespectacled individual, whom she recognises as Gary Sutherland, social historian and leading academic.
She has seen his face often on TV discussion programmes and
heard him on Radio 4 talking about changing social patterns. He
writes a magazine column and regular pieces for the *Guardian*
and the *Observer*.

He wanders over and she feels the force of his attention

directed at her and squirms. She isn't used to such close inspection. On this particular afternoon her legs gleam in opalescent black nylon and she is aware of his gaze sweeping them.

They become involved in a gender discussion that ends up in a bar and later in a date for the following afternoon – he doesn't mention evening. Well, of course he wouldn't because, as Emma discovers, he has a cosy wife and two well-bred children called Tobias and Alexandra, who do all kinds of arty-crafty things and play the violin and the piano.

None of this however precludes afternoon and occasional weekend encounters with Emma dressed up in suspender belt and sheer stockings and a waitress outfit in Gary's university study (locked door of course) or in Emma's flat or even in hotel rooms. She learns the wiliness of stockings, hears her lover's breath draw in sharply as his fingers glide from shiny stockings to warm naked inner thigh, and through his response she receives intimations of a bygone age with its multi-layers of intriguing sensuality that shift and shimmer.

She isn't sure where this will end either, but her stockings, like those of her long dead relative, Dora, or her Grandmother, Edith, have a special place in a small discreet drawer.

Reflections on a Shoe

You can measure your life in pairs of shoes. You're wearing new Clark's sandals and blinding white ankle socks. The tart odour of strawberries is in your nostrils, then comes the first chill bite and sweetness; long grass tickling bare legs. A scratch on the soft brown leather is unsettling and hurts like a bruise.

High-heeled black suede, peep-toe shoes come next – sling-backs with brocade fronts – crazy for a fourteen-year-old and bought with pocket money. You are in love with your feet, in the curve of sole meeting heel in a lovely sweep. This is a time of secret yearning for a boy, of dreaming of those feet walking towards a lover – only there isn't one. You never meet boys. Boys are a distant species. You attend a girls' grammar school hidden away behind dusty rhododendron bushes and where the only male ever to penetrate the mysteries is the withered caretaker, who has wobbly false teeth. Shoes for the girls' school have to be brown clomper lace-ups with low heels, round toes and no style. They are intended for school children and grown-ups with no imagination.

You swear to yourself that you will never ever wear brown clothes again once you leave school and certainly not brown shoes. None of the teachers has any flair. The music teacher mouses around in dark grey suede slip-ons with elasticated gussets, which merely look furtive. The fierce bolster-bosomed English teacher and her lover, the foxy-toothed French teacher, both wear flat lace-ups – no joy, no spark.

There isn't an opportunity for you to wear the passionate brocade sling-backs. They simply parade at home before your bedroom mirror. But then comes the sixth-form ball. You can't dance, though you'd love to know how. Some girls already have boyfriends and they produce these, stuck on their arms like handbags. You are unaccompanied like the strange lumpy girl, Enid, but you don't care, because you are wearing your brocade shoes and white dress (home-made by a friend of your mother and therefore a bit dippy at the hem) but embroidered round the neck with black sequins.

You exchange burning glances with the older brother of a girl in your class. He has pansy-eyes, longish dark hair, and wears black leather casuals. He moves towards you. The evening is you both together – the dancing isn't wildly successful but his hand on your waist and his voice telling you things compensate.

Then it's over – you never see him again but the encounter has thrust you into a romantic dream.

Running parallel with the brocade sling-back fantasy is another: art student in pumps or ballet shoes. You save up for some wine-coloured moccasins, leather soft as dough, gathered over the fronts by a drawstring into a gentle ripple like the edges of piecrust. They have leather soles and cut definite sounds on pavements. You have gazed at these in Saxone's window for an age. Now, to own them is miraculous. You have also managed to construct a long circular skirt from unbleached calico, and have dyed it purple, along with one of your father's cast-off collarless shirts. These, worn with a pink and purple chiffon scarf at the neck, make you think you are on the Left Bank (you have recently visited a French pen friend there). You are painting murals on your bedroom wall at this time (you have a very understanding mother), in fact painting every minute, and it is necessary to look the part.

In summer you wear pink fabric pumps with this outfit and you can transport yourself to the Louvre where you stare at 'Winged Victory' or Rodin's 'The Kiss' and then wander down boulevards shaded by plane trees; you nibble at a long French stick and smell garlic and scent and sometimes dark sewer whiffs from the Seine.

First term at university, and for a Going Down Ball you splurge part of your grant on a pair of impossible plain black-suede court shoes with four-inch stiletto heels. You touch them with reverence and stroke the downy surface, which caresses the pads of your fingertips like silk baby hair. You admire the plunging insteps. They are winkle-pickers and their toes form an acute point. Murder on the feet but exquisite. Sexy insane shoes and you wear them with a tight black sheath dress, shoulder-length white gloves and a white carnation frill against your shoulder. By now you have a boyfriend who wears black Chelsea boots or suave black lace-ups in fine leather and a pin-stripe suit for formal occasions. He has shown you how to dance – dancing pounds through your bloodstream now. Your black-suede stilettos are enclosed by his suave black lace-ups. He whirls you and turns you. You balance and pivot on those sexy, crazy shoes and you never want this to end and it doesn't for a long time. It is a world of stilettos stuttering and sliding over parquet floors and drinks in bars and Black Russian or Sobranie Cocktail cigarettes, reposing in black boxes like rainbow-coloured pastels.

You watch those suave black lace-ups pressing down on the accelerator pedal of his sports car and the wind tangles your hair and rushes in your ears and you recline, stilettos displayed in all their elegance.

You wear white satin stiletto-heeled shoes for your secret marriage. The dress is short and the sleeves and bodice of white lace and the gauzy skirt fans about your thighs. They let you sway and turn and twist in hot rooms with gyrating fellow students at your crammed wedding party.

Your graduation photograph shows you looking self-conscious, feet posed, right ankle crossed over left, to show off black T-strap shoes with illusion heels. These heels curve dramatically to their tiny base. They are a dream to wear, and as you trot across the stage at the City Hall to receive your scroll from the Vice Chancellor, you have no fear of stumbling.

Married life is going to be in the tropics. When you pack for departure, in your luggage are three pairs of patent leather sling-backs, which also fasten round the ankle with a thin strap – one pair is scarlet, one white and one blue. They too have sculptured heels.

Under brazen skies you wear the blue patent shoes and a turquoise silk shift scattered with mauve flowers, which moulds about your thighs as the hot wind blows off the marina. The shoes are more comfortable than sandals. Nor does the gloss on the patent leather succumb to the rapidly encroaching mould cultures which ruin other shoes. In the house you wear flip-flops and these display your scarlet toenails.

Then there's a war on and the streets fill with armed men and you're escaping in sandals, just strips of leather.

One day you discover those suave black lace-ups framing feet in high-heeled strappy sandals, and you know it's time to move on.

Back in England, on the day of your divorce your shoes are mink-coloured, kitten-heeled and suede with an ankle strap. Your long-sleeved dress echoes the colour of the shoes. You look sensible and ladylike and sad because a dream is over.

Thereafter things change. Never again are the heels so high. Your feet in trainers or ankle boots stride down echoing corridors and enter classrooms to stand before hulking apprentices. You have taken refuge in jeans and sweaters. Soon you become the wearer of plimsoles in summer. You buy knee-high leather boots for winter and long narrow skirts with a slit up the front.

The next time you marry, blue wedge-heeled sandals peek

through the folds of a long flowered cotton dress as you enter the registry office.

Nowadays you embrace the clomper shoes of your school days – and you mouse along like your old music teacher did in suede loafers with elastic gussets. But it doesn't stop there, you turn to Doc Martens, no longer fashionable; Doc Martens ablaze with turquoise and yellow flowers; blue Doc Martens, huge boots that cushion the soles and hold the ankles. In the massive Docs, striding is easy and there is no squeezing of the toes into constricting points to cause painful corns and bunions. You have spread out into your life. It is no longer rocking and passionate but grounded and tranquil and there is at last something you might call peace.

As the Shoe Fits

It was no accident that Kelly worked in a shoe shop: shoes were her passion and they had become so because of Cinderella's glass slipper. As a little kid she had tottered before the dressing-table mirror in her Mam's stilettos. If Mam or the Aunties caught her, they'd laugh – well, the Aunties would, but Mam would go mad.

'For goodness sake, Kelly, you'll ruin my shoes!'

None of them had ever understood Kelly's pleasure in touching the long, spiky heels and the pointed toes, and her enjoyment at the way the shoes plunged down at the front. Mam's feet and legs suddenly appeared different when she wore her black suede stilettos with the diamante bits across the front. They were glamorous and didn't belong to Mam, who often wore pink or blue plastic sausages in her hair and slobbed about the house in slippers with blobs of fur over the toes that made you think of hairy caterpillars. At such times her legs became clothes poles.

First Kelly landed a job in a cheapo shoe shop, where the leather felt like sandpaper and soon went scabby and a lot of uppers were made of plastic. She couldn't bear plassy shoes. The men's shoes had bumpers round their fronts like those on dodgem cars or were vomit-coloured brogues with thick composition soles. All the shoes looked unfinished. The male customers were oldies, the sort who wore Fair Isle zip-ups under buttoned up jackets, or lads being bullied by their mams who moaned that the kids would be through the shoes in a fortnight, which they often were. And then the complaints would start.

The manager, a real clever-clogs, made the women feel they were liars and it was their fault that the shoes had caved in. Kelly hung back during the complaints because she felt embarrassed. It was the awfulness of the shoes, though, which made her decide she must find another shop – she wanted quality shoes.

She could hardly believe it when Hunter's took her on. It was a very snobby shop, where the assistants had to keep their voices down and always smile sweetly even at snotty cows who'd have you fetch half the shop out, window display as well, whilst they preened and posed and pouted at their feet. In the end women like that always said, 'I think I'll leave it, dear – that wasn't quite what I had in mind.'

The shoes themselves, however, were fantastic. They were made of the finest leather and everything about them looked expensive. They were shoes to make you dream.

Kelly and two more girls and the manageress were in charge of the whole shop, which hid in the middle of a new shopping mall, and yet everyone knew where it was. It did not need to advertise. They sold only men's and women's shoes.

Now apart from adoring women's shoes, Kelly had this other side to her passion: she couldn't help watching men's feet and thinking about their shoes too, and in fact her interest in men's footwear surpassed even that in women's.

She liked to stand gazing at the black leather casuals with the gathers over the instep, or the narrow dark-brown brogues, or best of all at the black lace-ups with the thin soles. These shoes were sly wily and elegant. Men like John Travolta would wear them. They'd have thick black hair that rose in a wave from their pale foreheads and was gelled back, and brilliant black eyes, and they would give you a single red rose, and worship you, and yet be tough – yes, strong and tender. Men in dark suits with wide shoulders and narrow waists who carried leather executive cases wore these, and they drove Porsches as shiny and black as their hair.

The glass slipper had waited for Cinderella – that was amazing. There was Cinderella with the feet she'd had all her life, and only she could get her toes and bunions into that particular glass slipper. And that was how it was with the thin-soled black lace-ups. They were waiting for the prince to come, and they stood side by side on a sloping glass shelf, just biding their time.

Some day the prince would arrive and like Cinderella he would take the shoes from the shelf and try them on and then … It was through the feet that you could identify people. Kelly had sussed that out long ago.

Mam often dingled off to Mrs Greaves, the clairvoyant, or got Aunty Jean to read her tea leaves. Kelly believed you just had to study people's feet. When Mam had been involved with that Brian, who wore dodgem shoes, she knew it wouldn't be any good and wouldn't last, though Mam needed Mrs Greaves to tell her that.

Sometimes if you looked at people's feet, you saw this other person trying to get out. There was this fuddy lass with pink NHS specs and one of those camel-coloured macs, belted of course – the sort who wears jumpers and skirts. You would have expected her to have Hush Puppies on her feet, but no, they were sandals, stilettos with sling-backs – made her feet real sexy but they didn't match the rest. And there she was clopping round and nobody would ever know – well, of course her special person might identify her, her Mr Right.

Brown shoes would be difficult – the worst were the ones with square or slanting fronts that were meant to be healthy. The men who went in for those would eat beans and seeds and disgusting things from health-food shops and wear blue anoraks or green waxed jackets. Ugh! Oh and of course white Aran sweaters. But the completest no-no must be socks and sandals. When men hoofed in with grey or white socks poking through marmalade-coloured sandals – well – they were in the wrong shop. That was all you could say. Generally they would just peer about not touching anything and then clear off. The only time they showed any interest was if they saw a sale sign, which wasn't often.

Because Mam couldn't understand the importance of shoes and never had been able to, she thought that Shane was 'a lovely lad', 'real polite' – okay, maybe he was, but he always wore these massive trainers that looked like the hoofs of shire horses. They had once gone to see some shire horses working on a farm near Whitby, and Kelly had been comparing their feet with Shane's all the time. His trainers plonked down squarely and there was nothing at all sexy or intriguing about them.

'Why don't you get some real nice shoes,' she'd suggested.

'What's wrong with me trainers?'

'Well, they're just trainers – no style.'

He didn't know what style was – he wore his 501s and his rugby jerseys and that was that, and Shane wasn't the sort who would change. Shane was Shane.

Before Shane there had been Andy, who wore baseball boots, and Jason, who practically went to bed in his Travel Fox. Well they were nice and expensive and they did have a style, but somehow they didn't have any mystery. They bundled up Jason's feet – there was nothing sly about them.

All these shoes. She was staring away at the feet of passing males as they pootled past the doorway on a Thursday near Christmas – only twenty-one shopping days left – when these navy-blue slip-ons with a tassel on the front approached through the criss-crossing of boring trainers and plastic lace-ups. They entered the shop. The leather gleamed but not too brightly. They were seducer's feet. At clubs when the lights blimped and the music grunted and raved, you would sometimes glimpse a girl's feet in stilettos enclosed by two shoes like the tassel ones.

AS THE SHOE FITS

You were told not to pounce on the customers; on the other hand, you must not leave them to stuff their bags with shoes and hare off, or lead them to snort in disgust because they thought they were being ignored. You had to watch them discreetly and then approach, smiling fit to crack your face.

'Don't swamp them,' the manageress lectured during staff training. 'If they feel cornered, they'll bolt.'

She made you feel you were fishing, dangling your rod and line over a stream – that nasty Brian of the bumper shoes had always been on about maggots and playing the bait.

But the manageress's bottom line was: 'Girls, you've got to sell – trade's bad, they'll close us down if you don't.'

The other girls, Julie and Steph, had spotted the tassel man too, and while looking at their nail varnish peeked at him and gave these knowy little smiles.

He didn't bother at all with the reduced rack. That clearly was not for him. His eyes were seeking something and he wasn't going to spend ages dithering. Men tended to be much more direct than women anyway. For a brief moment he stood by a display of slip-ons; picked one up, stared at it, put it down. Now he moved towards the thin-soled black lace-ups – those mysterious, powerful shoes. He removed one from the sloping glass display unit and turned it over.

Kelly knew the feel of the leather; it was pliant and quite soft. As it wore, it would perhaps wrinkle slightly but that wouldn't matter. You would be able to tell the shape of the feet inside it – they would be elastic feet with a high instep; feet that would ease down on accelerator pedals, but nothing too quick or jerky.

And he handled the shoes, Kelly found she was holding her breath. A real common type tried to get her attention about some hefty black boots, but she didn't want to notice, let Julie deal with him.

'Have you a nine in these please?' he asked.

A nine! Yes, she had always thought that nine would be an ideal size, a nine in black lace-ups. As she passed amongst the tunnels of black shoeboxes, searching for the dream shoes, her heart capered – the glass slipper, here it was.

She hardly dared to look at the man as she handed him the size-nine shoes.

At this point, as Cinderella let her toes creep into the glass slipper, the prince would be struck by the amazing realisation that he had found his true love. All those other feet with hammertoes and bunions and in-growing toenails; the threes and tens and sixes – none of them was right for him. But now in this moment as Cinderella's blue eyes met his, he knew that inside her humble tatters there was this princess, his bride.

The man didn't speak to her, just nodded and took the shoes. He was wearing navy-blue socks, which exposed an inch of tanned ankle as his trousers slid back.

He fastened the laces and then stood up and paced back and forth gazing at himself in the long mirror. His aftershave, which might have been Rapport, wafted her nostrils. It was all wonderful ... wonderful. Kelly was struck dumb with wonder. It amazed her that Julie and Steph could carry on preening and burbling their usual: 'Now can I tell you about our special suede protector. You need to spray the shoes once before going out in them, you know, or they might get marked. Oh, and it only costs £2.75. This is a new one on the market and very good. And what about shoetrees? No – well, you need to keep your shoes in shape you know.'

All that blether and they couldn't see that something amazing was happening – love at first sight. It told you in *True Love* and *True Romance* about this instant, overwhelming attraction where eye meets eye – only here it was eye meeting feet – still, that made it more unusual.

'Yes, these will do,' he said.

Kelly jumped because she hadn't expected him to speak and certainly not say something so mundane as that.

'Oh fine,' she said and smiled at him. His mouth twitched a bit. He was wearing a navy-blue suit, a white shirt and a plain navy tie, and he had a black leather executive case in his hand. No dirt or raggedy broken bits spoiled his nails. They were pink and filed straight across. He took her breath away. She stroked the shoes into their black box and folded the dark-chocolate paper over them. They were very handsome. And now he walked out of her life with his shoes in a black plastic bag with Hunter's written across in gold script.

'Thank you,' he said as she gave him the receipt. He put it into his wallet and slid that into his inside jacket pocket. His movements were very sure and controlled and they mesmerised her.

'Kelly, can you serve, please?' the manageress squeaked.

After that, the day crawled by and Kelly could think of nothing else but the man with the black lace-ups, and the moment when he had tried them on.

It was Christmas Eve and Julie and Steph and she had pinned pieces of tinsel in their hair. Shane was supposed to be taking her out for a meal and to meet his parents, but she wasn't looking forward to it. Ever since the day of the prince she had been feeling low. Whenever she walked through the shopping mall on her way to and from work, she looked for him, always thinking that she might glimpse him in the crowd, though she never did. But then on Christmas Eve he strode in, pushing the plate-glass door open.

Kelly was about to fetch another pair of black ankle boots for a perfect cow of a woman, who'd tried on every boot in the shop, and was pursing her lips and twisting about, glancing over her shoulder as she pranced back and forth before the mirror.

'No, I don't feel exactly right in these – I don't really think they're *me*, and what a price! I mean, they aren't cheap, are they?'

What was she supposed to do? It wasn't as though she owned Hunter's herself. Oh God, there he was – he was coming towards her. He must have realised …

'Excuse me,' he said.

'Oh yes,' Kelly purred, using her creamy, little-girl voice.

'These shoes …' He extended the black plastic bag towards her. 'They're flawed.'

A coldness swept over her. She took the bag to the cash desk and brought out the shoes. Of course the man was right. She noticed a small hole where the uppers were coming away from the sole.

'Hi, Howard,' the woman with the boots cooed; she was a proper cow. 'They charge enough, don't they?'

'Yes,' he said, 'substandard stuff as well.'

Kelly noticed that his dark eyes bulged at her and he had a cold snappy face. She didn't like the way he touched the shoes with the tips of his fingers in prissy distaste. His chilliness terrified her and reminded her of the headmaster at her last school. Twice she had been sent to his room for being cheeky and once for truanting. Miss Jones had spotted her in Boots when she should have been in maths. The head had looked at her as though she was something nasty on his shoe.

'I'll have to fetch the manageress,' Kelly told the man.

'Yes, you had better.'

What a prat! She couldn't get over it.

There was something of a scene and the man had to fill in a form. The manageress said he must have cut the shoes on something, but the man said he hadn't and she was making excuses for shoddy workmanship.

When he had gone, the manageress said, 'Well, I'm glad to be shut of that one.'

It all cast a blight over Christmas Eve. Kelly felt puzzled and didn't know what to think.

On arriving home, she put on a new black dress that she had bought with her last wage packet. It was 'figure-hugging', the assistant had said. She gave herself a good spray with Mam's Poison (a present from one of her hideous admirers) and tried to cheer up.

'You look a proper treat,' Mam said. She was off out with her new man. 'Enjoy yourself, Kelly, love,' she said.

'Oh, I don't I expect I shall all that much.'

'Why ever not? What's up?'

She could not have said. It had been too unsettling, besides Mam could not have understood.

Just then the doorbell trilled.

'That'll be Shane.'

'I'll let him in, love,' Mam said.

Kelly went on glaring at her hair in the mirror over the gas fire, and fluffing out the blond question marks so that they twined down her cheek. Her hair was a regular bird's nest, she thought. Whilst she was still staring at it, she saw something through the mirror which astounded her. Some thin-soled black lace-ups were advancing. The sly seducer's feet halted behind her.

'Wow!' Shane said.

As they went out into the road, she began to wonder who this was – it seemed she had never really seen him before. He might do anything – a little shiver prickled along her back and down her arms.

Dressing Up

When Kim announced to Mam that she'd got a job in Cherry Ripe, the naughty knickers' shop, it was as though a bomb had exploded.

'You haven't!'

'Yes, I have; well, what's wrong with that anyway?'

'It's discustin' – don't know what your Dad'll say.'

Mam worked in an insurance office and wore crisp white blouses and full skirts in summer that bunched at the waist and dingled about mid-calf. In winter it was straight navy skirts and always safe navy court shoes and she toted her square navy handbag.

Dad painted and decorated for a living, but never liked giving their house the treatment. However, Mam insisted, and every year there'd be new flower-squiggled wallpaper springing out all over. Kim felt it was all so boring, so tame. She was sick of being bored.

On her way to school for years and years she'd been staring at Cherry Ripe. It had a green and red striped awning above the windows to shield them from the sun and she'd often see a woman poling away, letting the awning down on bright days.

When the bus ground to a halt close by it, all heads would turn, particularly male ones, and Kim had thought that the bus might even topple over, zapped down by Cherry Ripe magnetism. The lads on the school bus hooted and peered, and the girls wanted to look but restrained themselves because of the lads.

During the time when she'd been at school, supposedly wrestling with *Deutsch Heute*, Algebra and other sleep-inducing subjects, the thought of the shop had set her imagination skipping: what would you see if you went in? What if people spotted you entering? The woman poling the canopy up and down looked normal, maybe even a bit fuddy, rather like Mam. That made it more intriguing than ever. Perhaps they used the canopy to prevent people looking in; and it wasn't as though you dared linger outside.

A million folk stories had grown up around Cherry Ripe: they sold all manner of exotic lingerie – sexy, dubious things that you might see women wearing in the men's mags that Mr Towser, the newsagent, a medallion man, kept on his top shelf – titles like *Men Only* and *Mayfair*. There might be other contraptions too, stuff you wouldn't have heard of; all exciting and forbidden, hinting at perversions.

All men, Mam had always made clear, were dangerous rapists and monsters underneath. You had to watch out. Other lasses always said: They're only after one thing.

Basically school had not been for her. She'd taken to twagging in the last year and wandering round the shops with her mate, trying on tops in Miss Selfridge's, spraying herself with the perfume testers in Boots and having the odd fag.

Then came the 'schemes' and they'd been deadly – one in a greengrocer's where you got earth in your nails and had to lug boxes about; the other in a laundry that made you sweat and use tons of deodorant. So when she saw the ad in the evening paper for a sales assistant in Cherry Ripe – 'Must be personable' – she'd rung up straight away and been given an appointment, though she didn't know what 'personable' meant. This real sensible woman had interviewed her.

'Well, dear, you see we get all sorts coming in here, the customers that is – you have to be able to deal with.' Her voice trailed off, leaving Kim to speculate. 'You look all right though. I'm sure Mr King will think so.'

What did she mean? Kim was twiggy and had helped-on blond hair and was given to wearing black flares and black belly-exposing tops and looked about twelve, which annoyed her.

'Mr King's the boss, the owner, but we don't get to see him much. He has a gallery.'

'Oh.' (What did you do in a gallery?)

'Anyway, you'll be all right. I'll be here at first mostly. I'll show you how to carry on.'

Now, faced with Mam's forebodings and fury, Kim tried to look glum. Inside she was chortling and still running through the pictures of Cherry Ripe's interior. Straight facing you as you went in, and balanced above the glass-fronted drawers, which contained bras and knickers and other exciting things, were thigh-high black leather boots with six-inch stiletto heels, heels as thin and slick as daggers. She couldn't take her eyes off them and imagined herself prancing about in a pair on stage and singing whilst a group of black-haired, stunningly handsome men in evening dress closed in behind her and then swung her up in the sir. It would be great to be another Madonna, only different.

A message on the counter caught her eye. It said: 'Your fantasies begin here.'

Everywhere were show cards of women wearing lacy bras, who beamed shyly out at customers or looked sweetly serious. Then near the boots she'd noticed a poster of two blonde girls with smoky eyes, rather like herself, kissing and doing things to each other; what she couldn't tell. They were both wearing black dresses and not much underneath except for some G-string type efforts. Pushed to one side was another display card of two blondes but this was really a picture of girls' bums. Their knickers had got sucked into the crack between the globes. Just looking at these thongs made her feel uncomfortable, because they reminded her of being at school, and when your knickers were wearing out, they'd creep up and lodge in your crotch and chafe. It seemed daft wearing things that were bound to rub you.

Whilst she was still pondering about that, Mam was letting fly: 'You don't know. I bet there's some right oddments go in that shop – and I mean to say …'

'Mam, it's just like Marks and Spencer's really.' That wasn't strictly true, but still. If M&S didn't line all the underwear up on racks and if they'd had a few display cards, it might have looked nearer to Cherry Ripe.

'It's not for young girls,' Mam kept at it, 'it leads men on.'

Kim noticed that Mam's cheeks had turned pink. She felt a faint ripple pass over her, something that moved between fear and pleasure; 'leads men on', bloody hell! She pictured the buses swaying, all tilting at an angle as men cricked their necks trying to gaze into the windows.

'Well, it's better than nowt.' That was the trump card. Work was a very important word in their family. She often heard Dad rumbling on about 'scroungers' and 'If kids want to work, they'll find it. There's no such thing as can't get a job.'

Mam didn't like it but she was having to accept that for the time being Kim was forced to work in a house of ill repute.

'You'll have to try to get out of there as quick as you can, Kim. I daren't tell your Dad where you're workin'. He'd have a fit.'

So she was now going to penetrate the mysteries for herself. She'd always loved lacy pants and bras and here were drawers packed with cellophane bags each containing a folded bra.

As she approached the shop on the first morning, she kept peering about her, trying to be sure that no men were watching. Her cheeks blazed. She caught a brief glimpse of corselets, bustiers, teddies – all in white, scarlet, mauve and black – displayed in the window. A bald model was strapped into a black and white corselet, which sported two hearts over the crotch and fastened in front with two hooks. A lacy suspender belt and blue and white frilly garters held up the white stockings.

'Hello, love, come in!' Suzy, the chief assistant, mummied her. She wore a white blouse, black skirt and hairy black cardigan and didn't seem to fit in with the shop at all: Mam in her insurance office gear. 'Your name is Kim, isn't it?'

Kim nodded and smiled, her eyes zipping all over the place. On the counter she caught sight of another notice: 'Don't be afraid to give your requirements, nothing surprises us.' A shiver made the goose pimples rise on her back and forearms. What sorts of surprises were in store, because a notice like that must mean something?

During that first day she learnt what was in the glass-fronted drawers: lace-trimmed briefs and ivory-coloured silk bras with the thinnest of straps and matching silk pants; flowered French knickers in the palest blue, maroon and purple nestled in cellophane packets. They were made of slippery satin and had wide flappy legs that made you think of ladies in 1920s films; ladies in satin dressing gowns and with their eyebrows plucked into thin black lines above their huge sleepy eyes. She couldn't stop examining the merchandise. It thrilled her. The white whalebone corsets with hook fastenings right up the front made her laugh.

'I wouldn't fancy one of them,' she told Suzy.

'No, love, they'd be a bit warm I should think, particularly if you was carrying a bit of weight.'

Black PVC catsuits, trousers, minis hung on a discreet rail behind a display fixture.

'Oh, and we've got these, Kim,' Suzy said, slapping down some rubberised objects on the counter. There was a top, which looked like a skinny sleeveless T-shirt. Another package contained some pants.

'Bloody hell!' Kim said, 'what do they want them for? Must be that hot, and it smells.'

'They say it's the feel,' Suzy said, and wouldn't elaborate.

Kim ran her fingers over them. Yes, they did feel smooth, as smooth as flesh or silk. Obviously girls wouldn't be wearing such yucky stuff for their own pleasure. Anyway, they must look weird in them. But what kinds of men would buy this gear?

The first customer turned out to be a woman after a black 32A bra, which they didn't happen to have, but Suzy searched through the drawers and tweaked open countless packets to display their contents on the glass countertop. It all seemed quite nice and cosy and the girls on the display cards looked on, giving coy smiles.

After that the postman barged in with a parcel, which he banged on the countertop as fast as he could. He took care to keep his eyes averted from the display cards and the models and was in and out in a blink as though fearing an attack.

At midday a well-dressed man in a suit came in and approached Kim, who blushed. Suzy was having her nosh in the back.

'Good morning.' He had a very posh accent she noticed. 'I wonder if you've a red silk bra, 38C cup?'

Kim flurried in the drawers. There followed the ritual of getting out the boxes of envelopes, extracting bras and display-ing them on the glass. The man nodded and touched them with fine pale hands. No scarlet C cup. But he could have black. He took the black and three pairs of French knickers (large), all silk.

She folded them and slid them back into their packets. What would his girlfriend be like? Kim imagined a tall lass with great boobs and silky blond shoulder-length hair. Her scarlet nail varnish would be perfect and her diamonds as big as codeine tablets.

Just when she was slipping the lot into a green and scarlet striped bag, Suzy re-emerged from the back premises.

'Hello there.' She smiled at the man and he grinned.

'Not very warm, is it?'

'No, mind you, what can we expect when it's nearly Christmas?'

His pinstripe suit disappeared through the door.

'Somebody's getting a nice prezzie!' Kim said.

'Oh, that's for him.'

'You don't mean it!'

'Oh yes, he's a reg'lar; one of our usuals. Did I tell you, Mr King likes to know what we've sold and who to? There's a calendar in the back, best make a note of this one.'

'Why does he like to know?'

'Couldn't say.'

A succession of men followed but most of those seemed to be buying presents for girlfriends or lovers. They didn't look the sort who'd be getting stuff for their wives.

Just before closing time a big man with beer-coloured hair and nostrils like tunnels and bulgy brown eyes strode in. He was buttoned into a grey lounge suit. The shop vibrated with a deep spicy scent of aftershave. Kim noticed his heavy gold identity bracelet and his signet ring.

'Oh, Mr King, hello.'

'Everything going okay, Suzy?'

His eyes shot over Kim in passing and Kim's back and arms sprouted goose pimples. He was a wolf, she was sure of it. She thought of Mam's words.

'Yes, fine, Mr King. This is our new assistant, Kim.'

'Ah yes.' He didn't seem interested and went off with Suzy into the back to discuss something. Kim supposed she must have been giving him a rundown of the sales.

She continued to stare about her at the bustiers and packets of fishnet stockings on display. Beside her was a box of 'Dickie Bows' with the caption above them: 'Make sure your willy comes smart.'

Another box was labelled 'Chastity Belts for Men'.

After work Kim got home to find Mam frying the beef burgers and chips.

'How did it go, love?'

'All right. Suzy the other girl, well, she's a woman, shows you what to do.'

'There wasn't anything?'

Mam's thoughts were running on rapists and seducers, Kim could see, and it made her think of Mr King. 'No, nothing like that,' she said, 'just like any other shop.'

'Do take care.'

Every morning Mam said, 'Take care, mind how you go,' and gave Kim a certain look. It was the one that Dad couldn't interpret. She was also ready with the list of job vacancies in the evening paper when Kim got back.

Things had settled into a certain routine by this time. Kim was used to the mainly male customers; ones like the university lecturer with his frog-spawny eyes wriggling in the ripples of his lenses, who bought a waitress outfit, a black apron with a frilly white edge and a little white cap, black fishnet stockings and a black lace suspender belt. He just looked a bit nervous and intense during the whole proceedings of selecting the items and packing them in a plain white plastic bag. Others would stand there clopping a 10p coin on the glass counter and whistling to themselves to cover their embarrassment.

On this particular day, a Friday, late on, just before Christmas, Suzy whizzed off to do a bit of shopping, leaving Kim in charge. It was dark outside and she could see the neon legs and red stilettos winking on the sign in the window.

A group of fellers in their twenties hung about by the door, banging into one another and yelping with laughter. Kim felt a dither of fear. What were they getting up to?

Then the door opened. The gust of beery breath smacked her nostrils.

'Hiya, now then, Miss, have you got any, er …?' Here, the one speaking was nudged by his mate.

'Go on, ask her then, ger it out.'

They were red in the face with booze and excitement. Kim stared at them. They reminded her of lads from junior school. 'Yes?' she said.

'Have you gor any of them knickers with a hole in?'

Kim slid the crotchless brief box out. Privately she thought they were stupid. Your pubic hair pushed through the holes as though it had gone mad or turned into some furry creature.

'Fer the girlfriend.'

Then they wanted bras with nipple holes in.

'Your girlfriends won't want these,' she said, sounding, she thought, like Suzy, her voice quite flat. 'Bet you'll be bringing this lot back after Christmas.'

But they bumbled out on a wave of hilarity and beer, clutching their striped packages of crotchless briefs and nipple-exposing bras, apparently well pleased. Kim watched them lurching round the corner.

Two men in suits appeared and they bought diaphanous nighties and silk briefs.

No sooner had they gone than she saw the big form of Mr King. Her heart pattered. He'd only been in a couple of times since she'd started working there.

'Ah, hello,' he said, 'on your own?'

'Yes Mr King, I'm just about closing up.'

'That's right, you might as well call it a day now.' He let the Yale snap down and turned the card to closed. Kim saw an early slice of moon floating in the black sky, the legs winked. She felt nervous but she didn't know why. Mr King spooked her, though he was attractive in a weird way.

'How's it going, Kim?'

He had actually called her by her name and he sounded kind

and even interested. 'Oh fine, Mr King. Things are selling very well.'

'What things?'

She found she couldn't pronounce 'crotchless', so she rummaged in her mind for a euphemism, 'Oh well you know, the, er …' The word 'crotchless' expanded until it suggested rampant cucumbers and writhing pythons and she couldn't bring herself to say it.

'Yes?'

He gazed at her, lifting an eyebrow. His aftershave threw an aura about him.

'The briefs with holes,' she finished.

'Ah. What about PVC? Suzy tells me it's old hat now. The market's gone.'

'No, we've not sold much of that. It'll be too sweaty I expect.'

'Quite.'

She was about to fetch her coat, when Mr King stopped her. Was he going to pounce on her, drag off her clothes and make violent, painful love to her? She thought he must hear the clanging of her heart. They were standing very close to each other, but she only came up to the middle button of his jacket. He had on a charcoal-grey lounge suit with a white mac over it.

The world stopped as Kim waited.

'Would you like to do a spot of modelling for me, Kim?'

'My mother'll be cooking the tea.'

'It won't take long.'

'All right then.'

'Find yourself a pair of boots and a corselet. Make it red and black; whatever you like. Just get dressed up and then come out. I'll be in the back.'

It was fun getting into the massive boots, the red satin briefs and the black satin corselet, just like in some stage performance, but at the same time she felt a bit daft. What was he going to do? What would she do, if he tried anything on? One kick from the stilettos would disable a man, she decided.

When she tottered into the kitchen, he was sitting in an old armchair, warming his hands before the two-bar electric fire. A big black bag squatted beside him and a tripod had been set up. 'Just a few shots,' he said.

There followed what seemed like ages of poses, with Kim lying on the sofa over which a silky cloth had been draped, and kicking her legs in the air; or Kim bending down with her backside facing the camera and her face peering round grinning; or Kim leaning forward so her front popped out of her corselet.

Nothing was ever right first time. She must repeat the poses endlessly whilst the big black snout of Mr King's camera probed and pressed. It became part of him, thrusting, waggling. By this time she was covered with goose pimples because the little electric fire only took the chill off the air and, to add to her misery, the briefs had sunk into the crack of her bum.

'Just another couple,' he muttered.

It was whilst he was reloading his camera that they heard blows being thundered on the shop door and someone bellowing.

'Who the hell's that? You'd best get dressed,' Mr King instructed.

Before Kim had chance to change back into her own clothes, Mr King had been forced to open the shop door, and she came face to face with her Dad.

'What for buggering hell's sake do you think you're doin'?' Dad's face was brick-red with fury. 'And you,' he turned on Mr King, who was also very red in the face, 'you want lockin' up, you pervert! You'll have no daughter of mine workin' here. I could smash your face in! Get that muck off,' he snarled at Kim.

As Kim struggled out of the gear into her own clothes, she listened for the sounds of Mr King being flattened, but could only hear her Dad ranting on. 'You want closing down,' were her

Dad's last words to Mr King, as he marched Kim out of Cherry Ripe.

They got into Dad's van that ponged of paint fumes and he drove home, still fulminating.

'Your Mam was real worried, worried out of her mind. That's when she told me. Look at the time! Look at it!'

'But Dad he didn't do anything.'

'No, and by God, he'll not get the chance to either.'

Later when they sat round in the kitchen eating shepherd's pie, carrots and mashed spuds, Kim tried to explain but they weren't going to listen.

'Mam, it's not what you think. It's like playing games. It's just looking. They don't do anything. Nobody does things, it's just dressing up.'

'It leads men on.'

'It's perverted.'

Mum and Dad got quite excited about the dark and dangerous perversions of Cherry Ripe. In fact Kim hadn't seen them so animated for a long time. Why must they go on about SEX, hint, hint, as though it was some devilish number. It obviously wasn't if it needed tarting up so much. In fact it must be a downright yawn. Good job she wouldn't be working there any longer. Not that there was anything wrong with it, just that it was time for a new game. Cherry Ripe was cool, but it was no joke being stuck in the kitchen with old Kingy and being frozen for hours when she wanted her tea. Anyway it was all a bit daft.

In the job centres the buzzword was 'initiative'. Next time, she decided, she wanted something that would give her a chance to use her initiative, something a bit exciting. Maybe she'd have a nice dragonfly tattooed on her midriff and join a circus, or do skydiving.

The Gift

The problem about forming new relationships, Claire has decided, is that it requires a considerable amount of stamina. You have to work through a lot of information about yourself as though you were filling in a job application form for an academic post: d.o.b., childhood schools, attendance at higher education institutions, professional life, hobbies etc. But unlike this sort of information there is in addition the stuff about liaisons – and after a while this becomes quite a long list. So that's you – but then you have to assimilate all the same sort of information about any prospective partner.

As a teenager such things would never have occurred to her. Dave held her hand and could manage to mollusc his lips on hers and slip his fingers into her knickers without her ever wondering about his life; nor was he particularly interested in hers. In fact she constructed a personality for Dave, who in the end whispered away because he was more like a dandelion clock than a sycamore tree.

At eighteen she found Shaun and she slotted him into the misunderstood, much maligned category, a man needing sympathy and support to save him. But being a saviour, she has discovered, can bore you rigid, and anyway, such people don't really want to be saved. They have cultivated the habit of victimhood and enjoy nurturing it and become resistant to offers of help. And furthermore, they have a habit of trying to trample on you and turn you into a victim yourself.

Of course none of this has become apparent to her until much later.

Her thirtieth birthday traumatised her in some respects. Party time – big iced cake decorated with silver curlicues and 30 plonked in the centre; party poppers zinging through the air and 'Northern Soul' spinning off the decks, whilst her best friend, Mandy, leapt about and squealed, and she was courted by Jonathan, known since schooldays (no need to exchange d.o.b.s with him) and always written off privately by Claire and Mandy as a 'dweeb'.

'Well what's the matter with him?' Claire's mother wanted to know. Claire couldn't put it into words. Dweebishness consisted of an inability to be on other people's wavelengths; a lack of animation, humour – well, everything. The thought of him kissing her brought her out in goose bumps.

After that birthday with its sole dweebish admirer, Claire did some thinking – here she was at thirty having passed through a series of encounters only to end up alone.

Since that time, evenings of wine and hysteria have jittered by with Claire and Mandy discussing their present predicament.

'I just feel as though I'm not going anywhere,' Claire complains.

'You don't want to let that prat get you down.' Mandy is a stalwart who leaps out of bed in the morning grinning. She has a growing ambivalence to her present partner, a rough diamond, as she suspects he is turning out to be 'workshy' (her mother's expression) and a heavy drinker. 'I'm not carrying him,' she tells Claire regularly. 'Let him find some other sucker.'

Their careers hiccup along as a counterpoint to the relationship dramas on the home front.

'I feel stressed out,' Claire says most days.

'You aren't really,' Mandy's voice assures her, screeching down the mobile, 'it's lack of men – that's the trouble, that's what it is – you just think you are.'

'But I am – I think I'm sad.'

'Well there you are then.'

Claire's mother is at a loss. 'For goodness sake, when I was your age, I'd never heard the word "relationship" – you girls today seem to talk about nothing else.'

And then one Saturday evening Claire sees the man gazing at her in a bar. Mandy nudges her. 'Yes,' Claire says, 'I've noticed.'

Can he join them? Of course they say yes. You can't call him breathtakingly attractive but he has a way of asking questions as though he were really interested, looking into your eyes, and he sheds this aura of certainty about him. He wears designer labels and the sort of aftershave that makes you stare. All these details amount to something. She is intrigued. This just might be the one. Perhaps with this one they will both really *know* each other.

Claire and Mandy speak on the phone for hours. Whatever has happened hasn't really got any significance until they have dissected it.

This first meeting with Ed coincides with a worsening situation between Mandy and her boy friend, Al.

'He didn't go to work you know – was at the pub. Can't be doing with it. I've told him to go.'

'And what did he say?'

'Says he's not.'

'You'll have to change the locks.'

'It'll be too expensive – he's a real prat. I'm sick of him. You see I'm frightened he'll wreck the joint.'

The shadow of Al darkens everywhere. Claire receives a text message from Mandy at work alerting her to great dramas. Calling in on her way home from work, Claire finds Mandy blotchy faced. 'He's upstairs, says if I try to lock him out, he'll smash everything.'

Mandy's terrace house is her great love. She has spent weeks decorating it and it blazes with jewel colours and bead curtains that glimmer and chink when you brush against them. A jukebox dominates the sitting room where a leather sofa shocks with its whiteness – even the carpet is white. Mandy's is definitely a house where visitors must remove their shoes on entering.

They sit downstairs until four a.m. shivering and hearing now and then the sighing of floorboards and a voice grunting into a mobile phone.

After Mandy locks herself into the spare bedroom, Claire returns home, half-preoccupied with Mandy's crisis and half-cocooned by the new romance of getting to know Ed – Edmond Orlando Jenkins. What a name! Nobody else could have such a name. He isn't the usual macho, mouthy, deodorant-despising, inarticulate male, like Mandy's rough diamond, Al. Such men never say 'I feel' – instead they bang tables and bellow.

Ed is into Yin and Yang and says he feels it is valuable to explore his feminine side too. He talks as well about his 'inner child'. Claire is not sure what you do with your 'inner child' but it sounds quite exciting. His job is to listen to others stumbling through their life histories and this of course will mean that he is extra-sensitive, extra-caring.

Another definite plus for Ed is his choice of clothes: black leather trousers, a black fedora, black shirts or scarlet ones, boots – black ones that make the shivers trickle down your spine, black leather jackets. Even his mobile phone has class being so unobtrusive as to give an indication of its value.

Claire has had a passion for style all her life and Ed satisfies this. He obviously thinks of his image and cultivates it – Claire has not infrequently rejected the advances of men because of their footwear or their rigid tie/shirt/jacket appearance.

To match Ed's fashion interest, Claire finds herself spending an increasing amount of time and money in the shops on her way home from work. She has launched into a series of outfits: tiny skirts, dazzling vests, denim jackets, wedgies, shoes that shoot her up to the moon and accentuate the shaft of her legs.

He likes to frequent the casino, and on these nights she lolls at his elbow in a black satin strapless creation and silky black trousers that suggest the plump cheeks of her bottom.

That Christmas he presents her with a big silver box and inside it, wrapped in layers of tissue paper, she finds a jade dressing gown, a dramatic, sexy garment, which he hints cost an arm and a leg.

These sparkly days and nights have been rocking her along, so that she has begun to think she is in love. However there are drawbacks. Ed has a very tight schedule: 'I won't have any windows until the weekend.'

During the week his luncheon dates have been booked out well in advance, because he has a host of friends, both male and female, all of whom must be given his fullest attention. Only to sleep, to overindulge in wine, or to recover from a binge does he land down in his expensive flat.

On several occasions Claire, collapsing after a very tricky situation with the boss at work, has phoned him in tears, hoping to be consoled. He uses his professional counsellor's voice, of course, and seems to listen faster than she can speak – Mm, yes – yees – mm – but he doesn't bother to give her a cuddle. No, of course he is too busy.

Well, perhaps she is being unreasonable – after all his job requires that he listen hour after hour to people unburdening themselves about their unhappy relationships, work lives and neuroses. They must have drained him, she reasons – he is tired of listening. She wonders if all this listening and analysing of emotion leaves people blank and incapable of close ties. Surely not.

When she really thinks about it, she has to admit that he doesn't seem interested in her at all. His attention shuts down when she ventures onto anything about her early life. His way of escaping is by asking her a question about something totally unrelated, and in that way the focus of the conversation shifts. Though perhaps she is being too picky. She ought to leave things alone and stop wanting to pry.

Meanwhile the phone pings several times an evening and Mandy rattles on in high-voltage bursts.

'He's upstairs – says he won't go, no chance.'

Claire begins to detect a note of sympathy in Mandy's tone. 'I don't know where he'll go.'

'Well that's his problem isn't it, not yours?' Claire is surprised at the vitriol in her own tone. She thinks she sounds like Mandy – with Mandy it's always: There are loads more pebbles on the beach – don't bother with him. She doesn't understand why Mandy can't make the final severance. This scene with Al has been rerun several times, but finally nothing ever happens and they limp along for several more weeks after Al has sworn to reform himself. Of course he never will – at the time of swearing he has every intention of working and avoiding the pub but he quickly forgets and everything soon drifts back into the old pattern.

Claire hasn't heard from Mandy for a couple of days and assumes that she must have made it up with Al. Silence usually means some sort of truce.

Feeling rather low herself and cut adrift, as Ed is too busy to see her, Claire has decided on an early night and has just got into her pyjamas and the exotic jade green dressing gown when the door chimes alert her. She rushes to the bedroom window, opens it and peers down. Mandy is on the doorstep.

'Hi,' Claire shouts, 'just coming down.' This must be a crisis. Mandy stands damp and shaking before her.

'I had to get the police – he turned violent – they've taken him away.'

'They haven't!'

'Yes they have.'

Plug the kettle in; fetch the mad floral teapot. 'Toast?' Claire thinks that in emergencies toast is crucial.

'Oh go on then.'

Toast and raspberry jam in the middle of the night – but then Claire looks again at Mandy. 'I bet you've not had anything to eat for aeons?' No she's forgotten to eat. 'Right, well, omelettes.' Whilst Mandy embroiders on the drama of the police car swerving to a halt with its overhead light filling everywhere with glancing light and weird shadows and Al cursing and kicking out, Claire whisks up eggs. Oil smokes in the stainless-steel pan. She feels a sudden heat up her arm and across her back. Even her hair crackles. A raw bitter smell hits her nostrils. She screams and automatically shuts off the gas. She is alight. Mandy charges through from the next room. 'Oh god,' she shrieks and flings her anorak over Claire who chokes and sobs.

The whole thing is over in a gasp, leaving only an acrid stench of singeing.

Mandy is eventually the tea maker. They sit down together on Claire's second-hand sofa.

'That was horrendous,' Claire croaks. 'I could feel it burning my hair. I thought I'd be bald and it was running down my back and I just panicked.' She trembles with the terror of it still vibrating through her. 'I couldn't get over the smell. Think what it must be like for those people who set themselves on fire – and poor old Guy Fawkes. I'll never feel the same about bonfire day again.' She talks on, burbling and gasping.

Only by degrees does the trauma subside, and then her thoughts turn to the charred dressing gown abandoned on the kitchen floor.

'The belt must have been near the flame or something,' she says, 'but you wouldn't expect it to burn, would you, like that. I mean aren't a lot of pyjamas and dressing gowns meant to be flame resistant?'

Seized by the idea, Claire fetches her old dressing gown down from the bedroom, lights the gas ring and dangles the belt over it. The fabric smokes but doesn't catch fire. 'Look at that!'

'Must be some cheapskate job,' Mandy says, poking at the abandoned jade dressing gown, which Ed presented with such a flourish.

They return to the sofa. On this night Mandy's struggle with Al now over and the jade dressing gown having flared up like an incendiary bomb, Claire seems to see things afresh and starkly illuminated

They continue to sit side by side and then Claire slurps her tea and begins to giggle. Mandy joins in.

'Don't we look a couple!' Claire says, smiling at Mandy, whose cheeks are streaked with mascara and grief, and eyeing her own old sweatshirt and leggings – the garments she calls 'pyjamas'. Mandy grins back.

'We might as well finish the night off properly,' Claire says, getting up and fetching a six pack of lager.

Coats

In some stories coats have an apocryphal meaning, like the ones where a person, though in need himself (the person referred to in these stories is invariably male), gives his coat to someone even poorer. A coat is always the object donated – never gloves or a scarf or a jacket. It's easy to picture the coat as being tweedy and fairly nondescript – but it could easily be a long handsome narrow-fitting black one; or some flappy cashmere and wool caramel number. Such stories never tell you how the recipient felt. Was he embarrassed as the coat strained to encompass his girth? Irritated by the hugeness of it because it emphasised his own littleness – always a sore point? Depressed by the colour?

Sometimes the giving of coats can cause a major upheaval – take what happened in the case of two families.

Jade, for instance, is not your run-of-the mill kind of girl – in fact there is something seriously exotic about her. Her apricot-coloured skin makes you think of belly dancers in nightclubs, wiggling their middles in a serpentine way whilst coloured lights glance off their skin. Or she might be some South Sea Islander loping down a white beach shadowed by long-stemmed palms and about to plunge into the waves.

Though you wouldn't realise all this from the start because she looks quite tamed and prettied into her dress-shop role. She smiles at hefty women, wallets bulging with plastic, who let their equally robust daughters try on half the stock, splitting it on the way and then declare that, well, actually they've decided no thank you. All this done with a superior air intended to make Jade feel like one of the lower orders. It may be, though, that they don't notice her at all.

Other customers are so charmed by her helpfulness that they leave messages with the manageress about how pleasant it has been to shop in the store.

Jade has learned to fit in with the ladylike tone of the place. Well-bred women shop here. Shoplifters are easily spotted.

All the assistants have a choice from the stock for their daily wear and this serves as a subtle way of advertising the store's clothing.

So there is Jade, skirts skimming the knee and little matching jacket, her legs shiny in dark pearlised nylon, classy of course and restrained but hinting at something.

Off-duty she dresses quietly in attractive girly clothes, nothing too extreme. Skirts that demand she remain upright at all times or seated with legs carefully draped are not for her. Vic wouldn't like them. Nor would he like four-inch stiletto heels, or boob-revealing necklines. Colours must be reined in. Vic is her live-in boyfriend. Partner, she feels, would perhaps not be the appropriate word – well, she doesn't really know what to call him. They have been living together since she was eighteen and now she's twenty-eight and that seems a very long time.

When she first met Vic she was whipped towards him like a magnet to a fridge door. He is six foot four, the Viking type, though skinny and creaky-limbed as a praying mantis and with a long blond pony-tail. His hairstyle has started to cause problems because it limits the type of work he can do. He doesn't know the word 'compromise'.

They are not the sort of people who attend wild parties or who go clubbing or to rave-ups or pubs. Vic favours restrained evenings in their rented flat, eyes glazed with TV viewing. Every Saturday afternoon he takes root before sport on the set. Travel does not lure him either. He doesn't seem to be the sort of person who does things. He is content to spectate.

Jade accepts all this, though she finds his periodic moroseness difficult. 'I'm bored,' he often moans, 'bored.' She feels she ought to break out into some song and dance routine to entertain him, but she doesn't. It wouldn't work.

The relationship has endured for so long that there is no reason why it shouldn't continue. It has about it an air of permanence, of something unchangeable. But things are not always what they seem.

Jade's mother, Rosy, courts the unusual and the audacious. In one of her more zany moods she buys herself a long brown mock-fur coat. It has wide revers and a sweeping collar, great tunnel arms like wings that add to its impact. On arriving home, she realises that she is altogether too small in stature for such an imposing coat. Immediately she thinks of Jade, statuesque Jade. This is a Jade coat. She can see Jade striding along in it through winter streets with the hem brushing a pair of big boots. Jade would look stunning in this garment, a great princess.

So excited is Rosy by this picture that she phones her daughter at work. 'Found the most fantastic coat – too big for me, love, would you like it?' She describes its virtues, the curliness of the fabric, its sweep. She hears a note of caution in her daughter's voice. 'Well, sounds interesting, catch you later, Mum, somebody's just come in the shop. Have to go. Take care.'

Jade pops round to her mother's house after work. 'What about this then?' Rosy says.

'Wow,' Jade breathes in and then grins. 'Let's try it then?'

She stands before the wardrobe mirror in the coat admiring the way it drapes her body and kinks the air with excitement. This is not a nice safe little coat; no, it is an intriguing welter of a coat that bellows: Look at me! Jade falls into a dream of dervish music; of Northern Soul, rumbling and throbbing; of letting her body go in the liquid sound. She loves dancing. When she dances, she comes alive.

'What do you think?' her mother asks

'Way out – a dream.'

'Marvellous!'

Jade tears home, clutching the big black store bag. She sees people's gaze fix on the bag and then move to her face and they smile. She smiles back instead of frowning. Living with Vic, who is suspicious of everyone, has caused her to become equally withdrawn and reluctant to be friendly. He and she are together against an alien world, holed up in the stockade of their flat. But tonight something inside her is melting.

'What's that?' Vic's eyes swivel for a moment, leaving the TV screen.

'The most amazing coat.'

'Oh, where from?'

'Mum.'

'Why?'

'She thought I might like it.'

'How does she know?'

'Look!' Jade slips off her fleece and hauls the coat from its bag. Her fingers caress the heavy folds. She puts it on and twirls before him. Then she looks at Vic's face. His mouth twists with distaste.

'It's loathsome.'

Jade recoils as though he has slapped her cheeks. 'Well, I think it's brilliant.'

'I hate it – you can't wear that.'

They have one of their freezing stand-offs, where Vic retires into a deep sulk. These can last for days. He will not speak or meet Jade's eyes. She dithers inside and feels like a dried poppy-head with its seeds rattling in a stiff breeze. Such stand-offs are usually brought to an end by Jade declaring that she is sorry; she didn't mean to upset him; she will never do it again. After a period where she declares herself abject, crawls and accedes to his smallest whim, he lets himself be mummied round.

But this time isn't so easy. She nips loving glances at the coat and she tries it on when Vic is not at home. She admires herself in it. She is suddenly someone else, not the secretarial girly person in Vic's head. Somebody else, a bouncy, vibrant, sexy creature is trying to burst out – and this person doesn't work in a boring dress-shop. Conflicting urges give her migraines and palpitations.

The icy atmosphere continues with no let-up. Jade has stopped thinking about a thaw.

In this way two weeks go by and then one evening, quite late on, Rosy opens her front door and finds Jade there in her fantastic coat, together with four flight bags and several plastic carrier bags. 'That's that,' she says, and grins.

In the case of the second family, Samantha giving her daughter, Tracy, a leopard-skin coat has set off a dramatic chain of events, the repercussions of which will be felt far into the future.

Samantha belongs to that section of the community who decorate their houses once or twice a year, reposition their furniture and turn out the contents of their wardrobes with an eye to a new frenzy round the shops. In her wardrobe languishes the leopard-skin coat, a relic of her mother with whom she did not get on.

Tracy happens to be visiting her mother on the day of the wardrobe clean-out.

'Here,' Samantha says, 'do you want this old coat, it belonged to your Nana? I'm chucking it out.'

The coat has an opulence and sexiness which Tracy can't withstand. She pushes her face into the fur and sniffs. 'Sound,' she says. 'It's amazing.'

'If you like that kind of thing. Can't say I go a bomb on it myself. Too loud – common.'

Just the very sight of the coat has given Tracy an idea. That morning she has received a V.O. from her boyfriend, Tex, who is at present in prison.

'I am that fed up,' the letter said. 'I'm on twenty-three-hour bang-up and there's nothing to do but sleep. Food in this nick is crap – crap – soggy chips and a thing called rissoles that tastes like sludge. Come and see us, love you loads.'

She isn't allowed to take anything into prison and she has been puzzling how on earth she can cheer him up. The sight of the great cat coat with its funny splodges solves the matter for her.

One and a half weeks before Christmas and she waits to be let into the little boxy cubby hole where she will be able to see him through a wire-mesh reinforced sheet of glass. He has explained to her that this is to be a closed visit because of some incident in the prison. He hasn't of course explained what this is, but then Tex never does spell things out. There is always a mate, or this lunatic, and she can't follow the ins and outs of whatever is at stake.

Tracy sits wrapped in the great cat coat, eyes staring into the reinforced glass before her, waiting. Then Tex shoulders in. She gets a view of the naked lady scrolling up his huge arm. His blue and white striped shirt is open at the collar and she can see the broken lines of the tattoo round his neck but only the '-ut here' bit.

'Hello, love,' she says. 'How've you been?'

He mutters something which she can't hear properly and 'Nice coat!'

There follows a bit of conversation, which has to be limited to headlines shouting. Tex fumes about the glass. Then Tracy takes a deep breath and opens her coat. She poses naked for a fraction of a second and then closes it.

'Nice one!' Tex breathes and he is grinning fit to split his face. Time's up and Tex is led away.

Unbeknown to either Tex or Tracy, a prison officer has witnessed the scene and he watches the sinuous sway of the coat and the jiggle of Tracy's buttocks beneath it as she clops on her four-inch stilettos across the tiled floor. Smitten, he follows her to the exit and manages to exchange a few words with her. The blue of her eyes shocks him and the whites shimmer, her mouth blazes scarlet. He knows Tex Randle is doing twenty years for armed robbery and you don't mess with gangsters' ladies, but he can't help himself. He'll have to leave his partner, and from then on, who knows what will happen? There'll be dark shapes lurking round every corner.

Socks

Sometimes it is the triviality which proves to be the final straw. I read a while back the newspaper account of the judge who slew his wife because she moved the salt cellar two centimetres to the right – or was it the left?

So, it is the note centrally placed on the kitchen table which propels me into action. The note says: 'No clean socks. See you tonight. Love John.'

I stare at the words 'no clean socks' and a fury burns up my chest. No clean socks. This is somehow the end. I see John's dirty breakfast mug with the smiley face beaming at me from the draining board, and I seize it and hurl it at the wall and listen to the sound of it smashing, then I take a running kick at the shards of pot.

Socks, socks … it comes to me that socks have always been a malign influence on my life.

I was seven or eight and my mother consulted the calendar. Yes, May was out, we could go into socks, white ankle socks, new ones. Mine remained white for a few days, but the next time I wore them, they had become a stale dishcloth colour, which never changed. Now Miss Braithwaite stuck gold stars on the exercise books of girls with Persil-white socks. These girls also seemed to have shell-pink nails with cuticles pushed down to reveal paler crescent moons with no spiky bits protruding from the sides. Girls with dishcloth socks were treated waspishly. Indeed, I understood early that the colour of your socks reflected your status both in the class and for that matter in the world.

At the sight of the broken mug, I find myself moving towards the broom cupboard, but I stop myself. No, I shan't endure this any longer. I'll pack a bag and leave, just walk out, start a new life. This is a symbolic gesture.

But I am still preoccupied with Miss Braithwaite. I was probably still only about seven or eight and she was supposed to be showing us how to knit. The other children sat manoeuvring wool round needles and easing the needles through until they'd created a stitch. Sock making – I hadn't a clue – hated it, was bored by it. I scrabbled with the ball of wool, shoving it round the needles. I managed a couple of stitches and then dropped one and a hole appeared. Miss Braithwaite frowned. 'Just look how dirty you've already made that wool, Katie Wilkinson.'

Of course the sock was never finished and languished like some dead snake in my desk.

Schools seem to use socks as subtle tools of repression. My brother Julian was told that unless he wore knee-high grey socks he would not be allowed in the school. Our mother, not being the sort of woman who reacted well to instructions, took no notice until Julian was sent home with a stern note – then an embarrassing battle ensued.

Even the very expression, 'Pull your socks up', reverberates through those school years, reminding me of Miss Braithwaite's scorn. 'Kate Wilkinson, for goodness sake pull your socks up!'

Amy and Paul haven't got up yet. I can't let them see the broken mug. I dive for the brush and dustpan.

'Covering up the wreckage,' Paul says, 'I heard it.'

'Never mind,' I snap.

'What's up?'

He's a kid who will ferret if he senses a bad mood.

'Nothing – you'd better get moving or you'll be late and so will I.'

'Cool it, Mum, chill … no need to …'

Amy dawdles in. 'What have you broken, Mum?' she says.

'Dad's mug – she's broken Dad's mug,' Paul hoots. 'Nice one.'

'No big deal,' I say. 'Anyway, I must get ready for work – you two hurry up. If you aren't quick, you'll have to go by bus.'

I am still haunted by the curse of the sock and I can't let go of it. The kids poke around, unaware I'm in the middle of a crisis but sensing something. I feel like a sea anemone being prodded by children with a cane. My tentacles struggle to cover the soft centre underneath.

I shall leave him – this is really it.

A car horn pips outside the house. Amy wanders over to the window. No rush. The agitated pipping doesn't seem to disturb her at all. 'Oh,' she says, 'it's Jenny.'

'Quick,' I say, 'I'd forgotten, she must be taking you – hurry up!'

I rush to the door and mime thank-yous and won't-be-longs, whilst behind me a sluggish dragging of feet and a banging of doors indicate some activity. I put my head back in and bawl upstairs, 'Oh do come on, you'll make Jenny late.'

'Chill, chill …' I hear Paul muttering from somewhere in the hinterland. 'Can't find any socks.'

At the mention of the word 'socks' I am ready to burst. 'It's because you've never put them in the wash basket.'

Paul has Athlete's Foot and it leaves his socks curd-coloured and cheesy. Clean socks every day is the routine and liberal sprinklings with Athlete's Foot powder after foot washing – but he can't be bothered. I have to separate his socks from those of the other family members because I've heard the infection spreads like forest fire.

I can imagine the coils of discoloured socks strewn about his bedroom, just waiting for someone else (i.e. me) to muck them out.

'Oh well, I'll just have to go with stinking feet,' Paul trumpets as he stumbles out to Jenny's car, his backpack half off his shoulder, his trainers unlaced. Amy dreams along behind him. They've been arguing as usual, I can tell from the way they avoid each other.

'Bye Mum,' she calls and then slopes back to hug me.

Jenny sits at the wheel twitching with irritation. Her daughter pulls faces. I can't wait for them to be gone. Too late now to finish my piece of toast – the tea has a skin on it. The kids' mess of cereal and milk blobs and scattered corn flakes is stranded on the kitchen table covering the note.

They'll not be late – at least I hope not. I have an uneasy relationship with school. A scary area is the time last year when Amy fell at home one weekend as she rushed in her socks to clout Paul and skidded on the shiny cover of the *Radio Times* and went down hitting her head on the floor. The bang raised a big bruise on her forehead – it certainly could have been really serious but wasn't. Of course her teacher immediately thought of child abuse. Amy couldn't understand what all the grilling was about. I was stared at gravely on parents' evening. Tactful but searching questions zipped at me. How was my relationship with Amy; were there any problems etc? At first I didn't quite understand where this was heading.

Socks again – had Amy not been wearing socks on the day of the accident, it would not have happened.

I pull on a screaming pink V-necked cotton top and tuck it into the waistband of my black suit skirt. The pink is identical to the colour of the socks that Mark Andrews wore the first time I ever saw him. He'd just been appointed the firm's new supremo and was visiting the underlings, department by department. We were gathered in our office waiting, when he strode in – dark-navy suit of course – just another suited person amongst all of us in our black and navy suits. I suppose we all appeared almost to be in a uniform. But he stood out because of his hot pink and orange tie, no discreet little number here. After hauling himself onto a table, he sat there swinging his legs and that was when I saw his socks. They matched the tie exactly. His white hands gesticulated a lot in an eloquent way and he played it a bit joky, but he came on suddenly with the messianic stuff that elevated business to a religion. He must have been very sure of himself to sit like that – it made you think he knew what he was doing. The socks too were daring – men generally don't let themselves rampage with colour, particularly in a business environment; they play safe. He didn't need to. I found myself wondering about his underpants.

He talked a lot about the role of the entrepreneur, and how he was always on the look out for incisive thinkers and people who weren't afraid to take risks, and how he would reward such people – but if we failed, then we'd be out on our ear straight away. Even the swiftness of the promised retribution seemed sexy in an obscure way. We were all fascinated. The women dreamed about those pliant white hands; the men must have glimpsed some laddish quality in him.

Later we discussed him endlessly. 'God, I couldn't stop watching his hands.' 'Did you see his socks?' 'His legs were *tanned*.'

If he hadn't decided to drop in informally on all departments at odd times, to get an idea of what was really happening, he might not have noticed me … but that's not true – during the meeting our eyes did lock and it seemed he was speaking only to me.

I am still in that time of Mark Andrews as I shrug into my suit jacket, take my briefcase and flurry out to my car. He only had to look at me and I came scarily alive and everything inside me seemed to focus and a molten snag of lightning hit me between the thighs. Nothing outwardly had to happen. In fact all that summer the slow build-up stopped me from sleeping. I was caught in a magic mesh. Only I didn't know he was married and had been so twice before – or that he happened to be a hopeless romantic and given to serial relationships. Of course I lost my job over him – knickers in the glove compartment of his family car sealed my doom.

Mid-afternoon my secretary puts my mother through on the phone.

'Katie, it's your Dad – you know I can't get in tonight to see him – do you think you could call at the hospital on your way home, love?'

'Yes, Mum, fine,' I say, groaning inwardly because that means the kids' dinner will be late and, anyway, I don't like leaving them unsupervised.

As I drive into the hospital car park and buy a ticket from the machine, I start thinking again about packing a bag and walking out. At work I have been too busy to dwell on it, now it resurfaces.

Dad is sitting up in bed on the eighth floor. At the sight of me his face eases out. 'Oh hell, Katie.'

I kiss his pink cheek. 'How are you, Dad?'

'Fed up – look, they've made me wear these.' He hoiks up his leg. 'Socks … you have to wear these white sock things and they make me sweat and they feel tight. I don't want to wear socks. I told her I didn't want them and she said I had to – read the riot act – and if I didn't do what I was told and everything went wrong …' He rumbles on and I try to calm him down and reason with him, jolly him out of his irritation.

By the time I get home, Paul and Amy have already begun to witter about their lack of food. 'Mum, what about tea?' Paul greets me. 'Aren't we eating or anything?'

'Give me a chance,' I say. 'What about, Hello, Mum, had a good day?' He gives a sheepish grin. 'Well?'

'But I'm hungry.'

We have the usual exchange about how he should make himself some toast and jam if he's so hungry.

Quick change into jeans and sweatshirt and I'm frying onions and garlic and bits of bacon and mushrooms for a pasta dish and tearing up fresh basil. The kids drift about me, coming out with nuggets of information which they wouldn't if I were to ask them outright about their school day.

We're about to sit down round the table to eat dinner when I hear the front door opening and a gust of air causes the kitchen door to vibrate.

'Dad,' Paul pronounces.

I load John's plate with pasta and sit down.

'Hi,' John says. The skin under his eyes looks grey. 'Great pasta!'

At least he's got the good sense to be encouraging about the food.

'Got something for you,' he says, when we've finished eating and the kids have disappeared upstairs. He hands me a plastic carrier bag. I look in and see six pairs of entrancing socks: white spotted with pink hearts, stripy socks, joky socks patterned with giraffes and hippos.

'Thought I might as well get some for you whilst I was buying myself a few pairs.'

'They're absolutely brilliant,' I say. 'Now, before I forget, I'm giving a demonstration this evening for all residents on how to work the washing machine.'

He gives a mischievous smile. 'Okay,' he says. 'When does the demo start?'

That night as I'm falling asleep I remember I haven't got round to leaving John and I snuggle down with my head on his sleeping shoulder.

The Swimsuit

When Syd Burns handed his wife, Tanya, her birthday present, he asked her if she would come to the bedroom with him.

'I want to see you open it in there.'

'All right, love.' Tanya felt the oblong parcel. It crackled and its silver paper spotted with scarlet hearts dazzled her. 'I'm that excited.'

'Come on then!'

Once in the bedroom, Tanya peeled back the sellotape with care, whilst Syd waited, racing his fingers along the dressing-table top. Usually Tanya said 'No racing at Sandown' when he did that. Today she was too excited to notice. It was her big Five-O. The kids were due round later with their contributions. Dum, dum, Syd's fingers went. He would have had the paper off in a jiff. He'd spent ages choosing the present.

'Bloody hell,' Tanya said, 'eh, look at that.'

The foil fell away to expose the picture of a dark-haired girl wearing a silver swimsuit. Its cutaway legs revealed brown thighs with the glittering crotch nestling between them. The girl had one hand on her hip and her pelvis jutted forward, a swatch of brown hair sprayed her left shoulder. Her feet were posed in high-heeled strappy sandals. She smiled at the onlooker.

'Go on then, get it out, Tan!'

'Goodness me.'

Tanya eased out the silver garment. It felt like very smooth emery paper and yet was seductively soft. The touch alarmed and excited her.

'Well, what do you think?'

Syd always asked her that question. They'd spent twenty-five comfortable years together and were looked upon by friends and neighbours as the ideal couple. They took mutual decisions and didn't argue much. Syd was a family man and adored their three kids. Tanya's nets gleamed, her paintwork glittered and her Yorkshire puddings were puffball light.

'Oh, goodness me!' Tanya was still staring at the swimsuit, which she had placed on the bed.

'Put it on then, Tan.'

'I don't know about them legs.'

'Go on, give it a go.'

'I'll put it on in the bathroom, give you a surprise like.'

'Okay, but put a sock in it then, lass, we'll have the kids round next.'

In the bathroom amongst the avocado suite and gold-plated taps that Syd had managed to plumb in himself with much cursing and heavy breathing, Tanya wriggled out of her candy-pink leisure suit, white bra and pants. She started to insert her legs into the swimsuit. What a number! The cutaway bits revealed ripples of pinkish, piggy-looking flab and tufts of pubic hair that reminded Tanya of couch grass on a balding hillock. Bits of her squirmed out of the silver skin and would not be contained. She stood with her back to the mirror and tried to squinny at her bottom. Two large creased suety blobs squeezed the seat of the swimsuit into a silver string, which disappeared into the crack between them.

'Bugger me!' she said.

Meanwhile in the bedroom Syd stopped racing at Sandown and lit a cig. He sat down on the bed and let his thoughts run on a little frolic. The room was perfect, hot with late afternoon sunlight. Then his gaze strayed back to the girl on the packet. She was looking straight at him. Her cheeks had the golden-pinkness of a ripe peach. All of her looked succulent. He wanted to leave a love-bite on her neck, like he used to on Tanya's when they were courting. The girl's smile was very sweet; sweet and sincere and sexy all at the same time. The silver suit must have been painted on her. It emphasised the lovely swell of her breasts and made her legs look as though they reached up practically to her collarbone.

Tanya's mop head of grey permed hair and pink NHS specs shot round the door.

'I don't know about this, Syd,' she said.

'Come on in and show us then, love.'

'Er, well.'

'Oh, come on.'

His eyes encountered her bosom, which bolstered around her waist and oozed out at the armpits. They swam over the jellying of her thighs and here and there the mad blue squiggles of veining. He took a long drag on his cig.

'Yes, er, yes.'

'I couldn't wear this out, love.'

'No, nor you could.' His tone was flat.

'I'll have to take it back, love. Sorry about that.'

'Don't bother, I'll give you the cash. Just give it here. I'll see to it.'

Tanya was surprised but she didn't argue with him. What could he do with a swimsuit like that? Syd restored the garment to its packet, looked at the smiling siren and lumbered off downstairs, leaving Tanya staring at herself in the bedroom mirror. She saw this tall slim girl standing by her side; this kid who caused her own hips to look like sugar-pot handles and her face an ordnance survey map by comparison. The lass still drifted around. She unsettled the day and made Tanya's new tricel trouser suit all wrong. When had this wattly jaw and the slabs of flab stolen up on her? They had appeared without her ever having noticed, because she was always so busy. The day grew spiky.

She wished they hadn't planned the family party.

The kids gusted in, hugging her and filling her arms with parcels. She noticed how Syd didn't say much and confined himself to deep glugs of his whisky glass. She kept her fingers away from the three-pound Cadbury's milk chocolate assortment box, which someone had bought her.

After the day of the big Five-O everything began to change. For one thing Syd bought himself a new black leather bomber jacket, a pair of black jeans and some cotton polo necks. But most amazing of all, he returned one Saturday afternoon with a gold sleeper in his left ear.

When their sons brought their live-in girlfriends to the house, Syd chatted them up and gave them long cuddles as they were leaving.

'Me Dad's shaking a leg,' Darren, their eldest son, remarked, when he noticed Syd's earring. 'You want to watch out, Mam.' They all laughed.

Tanya smiled grimly; she saw again the silver girl on the swimsuit packet.

Syd saw the silver girl too. He'd be high up on his ladder undercoating window frames when he might glance down and spot the girls going by, girls with long dark hair blowing in the wind and skintight sweaters, thick belts pulling in tiny waists, and blue jeans to show off their endless legs. They rocked on platform heels or stilettos and opened their scarlet lips to screech with laughter and they lolled against each other over a private joke. He saw their flawless peachy skin and he couldn't stop staring. Which of them would fit into the silver swimsuit? At times he came within an inch of plummeting to earth, so transfixed was he by the sight of them.

He took to having pints in city-centre pubs where he hoped to catch sight of the silver girl again. Sometimes she was perched on a barstool and he would be presented with her sweet young profile and her upward-tilted breasts. Her red lips gleamed, her white teeth flashed as she smiled.

On leaving at eleven o'clock he'd glimpse flocks of exquisite creatures all hovering at the entrance to LA's, the central nightspot. He fixed on white blouses, long shiny legs and wiggling bottoms, and his nostrils twitched with the aura of scent and the whiffs of underarm deodorant and hair gel. Oh what intoxication!

Once home, he'd go to his garden hut where he kept his tools, lawn mower, any spare paint tins and his decorator's equipment. There he opened the second drawer of his steel cabinet and lifted out the packet. The silver girl smiled at him. He took out the swimsuit and let his hand run over it. She stood before him, his silver girl, flicking her thick dark hair over her shoulder. Then Tanya called, 'Cooee!' It was time for cocoa and sandwiches. He didn't want cocoa and sandwiches; he wanted to be at LA's leaping wildly to the twanging of electric guitars, whirling his silver girl round and round and feeling her hot breath on his neck.

'Do we always have to have this?' he snarled at Tanya. She shot him a dense look, which he couldn't be bothered to interpret, and didn't answer.

Shortly after that he stomped off to bed.

Tanya's life too had not remained untouched by the silver girl. 'I feel as though I'm just about ready for me twilit home and me bath chair,' she confided in her neighbour, Babs, after the fateful Five-O day.

'Why don't we get off to that step-aerobics and then have a sauna?' Babs suggested.

Before she knew what, Tanya was on the back row of the ladies in leotards, plopping up and down on her step. She thought her hamstrings would snap but she persisted. Then came the luxury of sitting on benches in the swirling steam, turning a shade of lobster and thinking of the handfuls of flab, which must surely be melting away. Step-aerobics three times a week, sauna, swimming; no more chockie bickies with mugs of chocolate. She was measuring herself against the silver girl.

Next she went blonde, a dizzy white blonde, and she bought some gold hoop earrings. She gave herself long appraisals in the wardrobe mirror. Sure, she was no teenybopper, but she observed that a certain raddled charm was emerging. It created its own intoxication. She began enjoying the windmilling of her arms and plopping up and down off the step and watching the teacher prance back and forth. The music and the voice set up a mesmeric pattern.

One day on the back row with her, she noticed a chap who looked as though he'd had a tractor driven over his face. His diamond eyes squinted and his voice grated. It had a deep gravelly honk.

'Hiya, lass, you've a good leg on yer,' he said when they came to the end of the session and stood steaming in the back of the hall.

'Is that right?' she said, giving him her red-lipped beam.

'Yer, you have an' all. Goin' in the sauna are you?'

'Yes,' she said, 'me and Babs.'

'Join you then.'

So they sat in the steam on the wooden benches and the man yarned.

'Oh, yer, there was this maharaja. He had a diamond as big as an egg on his turban.'

'Is that right?'

'Don't you believe it then, Tanya?'

'Course I do, Sam.' They were on first name terms by now. Sam's tales made her forget to vacuum the stairs and clean down the paintwork. She didn't bother to make Yorkshire puddings either, there was no time. She even forgot about the ham for the eleven-fifteen cocoa and sandwich routine – anyway, she'd given up on that, it was flab inducing. Now there were days of tropical heat in the step-aerobics emporium and the sauna and swimming pool. Limbs in shiny body stockings flashed; music pounded; the beat juddered and thumped like a mighty heart; sweat blistered on faces. In the sauna the heat intensified. It was all heat and moisture and slipperiness and tales of white temples and people being beheaded and snow gleaming on jagged fangs and dead bodies being pecked to white bone by vultures with tattered wings

On a Friday morning Syd, up his ladder painting away but always on the alert for the girl who would fit the silver suit, happened to glance down. There below him were two people who shocked him for some reason. He must look again. What was it that arrested his wandering thoughts? They were laughing together, laughing uproariously and they had a curious vividness about them that made them stand out from all the other passers-by. The woman's candyfloss hair shimmied in the breeze; the man had a craggy shape like some all-in wrestler. They both had faces you wouldn't forget – and yes, yes, it was Tanya.

His heart gave a great dong and he almost tumbled from his ladder. He wanted to shout but stopped himself just in time. For the rest of the day as his brush worked, slapping on paint and smoothing it, he fought the urge to rush home. He was angry. His head ached; his hand shook, so that he had to wipe up splatters of paint. What the hell was this?

When he was finally at home, washing himself in the avocado bathroom, he didn't know how he was going to broach the matter. He wanted to look at Tanya properly. He somehow felt he hadn't got a hold on life anymore. Even the bathroom taps looked dull and there were soapy splatters on the window. Something had happened whilst he hadn't been watching. It alarmed him. He decided not to go to the pub; better stay in.

Tanya put his microwaved dinner before him.

'Where's yours?' he said.

'I'm not having any, love.'

'Why not?' he stared at her now. Her hair was different, her earrings, her lipstick. She was somebody else. It bothered him.

'I've had mine earlier on.'

'Oh.'

'Aren't you off out then?'

'No.'

'Right, well, I've to go out. Thought as you'd be out anyway.'

He heard her moving about upstairs and then she shouted, 'See you, love.' And he heard the gate click. Gone. He picked at his Bird's Eye dinner for one. Later he sat before the telly, not really seeing anything, just staring at the jittering figures. Eventually he blundered out to the hut. For some time he messed about, putting his paint tins straight, aligning his jars of nails and his colour charts. Then his eyes fell on the shears he used for trimming the privet hedge. He had sharpened them recently and they had gleaming grey blades. He wrenched the second drawer open in the filing cabinet and hauled out the silver girl, then he hacked her to pieces. Scissoring the blades across her neck, her pert mouth, until the hut floor was covered with fragments of silver cloth and paper.

The kitchen light flicked on. She was back. He waited for her to call 'Cooee' but she didn't.

The Red Dress

Brian remembers quite clearly how his love affair started. Monday afternoon, five o'clock special cinema prices, he was installed midway down the auditorium – aisle seat – so that he could splay out his legs. He always made for that particular seat and felt cheated if someone snatched it first. He licked his Cornetto. The crunchy chocolate outer layer blended with the sweet white vanilla ice cream and made his saliva run. Oh, the relief of having escaped the College's echoing corridors and the flocks of whooping students. He had to be in position before the adverts, otherwise he would not feel satisfied. On that day the usual ads slid across the screen, mostly for cars, cold-sore remedies and body sprays. And then he saw her.

A young chap was hitching a ride in the back of a pick-up – obviously some Deep South scenario. He dropped off before a leggy, rickety building and climbed some steps to knock on the door, and this cinnamon-skinned girl in a scarlet dress greeted him. The dress sheathed her body and followed its contours until it broke out in wild froth about her calves. Her dark eyes and her wide mouth smiled. They danced on a Mississippi river-boat – well, he assumed it must be something like that – black water and the boat mazed with lights rocking upon it like an effervescent roman candle. The girl and the young man stood at the bar. Her buttocks curved mesmerically under the shiny red material. A trumpet solo raved and sobbed.

Afterwards he couldn't remember what the film was about, he simply wanted a rerun of the adverts so that he could see the girl in the red dress again. He took to going to the five o'clock performance every Monday, no matter the film, until the cinema stopped showing the old advert with the girl in the scarlet dress.

Ever since that time in the cinema, Brian has been caught in a dream of the girl. Of course the dream gets jostled by the everyday College rabble, but it still remains clear in outline and vibrant.

Enrolment day at the College and trestle tables line the big hall. Lecturers have their subjects posted up behind them on the wall. Above Brian's head a poster in uncertain letters advises: Communications. This will be a long haul. They are expected to man the positions all day long and into the evening.

Janet and Ellie have taken up residence by his side. They are the sort of women who bring in plastic lunch boxes sprouting with lettuce, cucumber, tomatoes and watercress and containing little sandwiches which they lift out from carefully greaseproof-wrapped packages. He glimpses the producing of lunch boxes from unsexy bags and gives a silent groan.

'How about a sandwich, Bri?' Janet treacles. 'They're Brie and watercress – the bread's stoneground organic.'

He's got it in mind to slip out to the canteen for a plate of chips but he daren't mention it. They will expect him to stay put.

''S all right, Janet, thank you.'

'Are you sure? We don't want you collapsing on us with starvation.'

'That's not on the cards, Janet.' She will continue to fuss and won't take no for an answer.

Eventually they turn their attention to the contents of their lunch boxes and he thinks he hears Janet's teeth squeaking on cucumber. There is a steady slither and scrunch as she masticates lettuce. They are launched on a discussion of the Head of Faculty. 'And she called him into her office – and …' Brian stops listening. The Head is too terrifying and he is not her favourite person. Part of him wants to hear her latest exploits but the rest of him has a superstitious belief that, by doing so, he will be forcing himself into the line of fire.

'When you think what she earns – and what does she do all day long? And those suits – well of course she had it off with the last principal – didn't you know?'

Brian decides that he will call in at the curio shop on the way home if it isn't too late when he finishes work. He has seen what he thinks is a genuine Art Deco figure, a naked woman supporting a lamp. As a collector of figurines he has several exquisite white marble women, reproductions of Greek statues. In fact his thin slice of terrace house is crammed with all manner of finds: marble cherubs; Art Deco coffee services and plates, all ablaze with orange, yellow, cobalt blue; Arthur Rackham prints – he has a fondness for the Gothic and the thorny; Victoriana with its sentimental gold-ringleted little girls and boys and big-eyed women; china chamber pots emblazoned with twining flowers. Dust shrouds all these trophies, as he never gets round to wiping them down.

Long boring interludes stretch across the afternoon, interrupted periodically by the appearance of gaggles of youths who have failed their A-Levels, or out-of-work women pushing buggies containing toddlers who crash through conversations with their squawking.

In the lulls Janet and Ellie do a hatchet job on other members of staff, but as a counterpoint to these run whispered bits about illnesses below the waist which are not meant for his ears. He lets himself fall into a dream of a girl in a scarlet dress. He is out on the Mississippi steamboat in a tropical night. He holds her against him and the smell of frangipani tickles his nostrils, his fingers touch the slippery slide of the dress. The music weaves them together.

He is shocked out of this riverboat idyll by a girl in a red dress who has positioned herself before his table and is staring up at the word 'Communications'. Janet and Ellie haven't noticed her because they are involved in some discussion about a thing called a 'coil', an object which appears to cause terrifying symptoms. 'Oh yes, it was terrible, flooding, you know.' Ellie's eyes shoot wide open.

'I think I have to come to you,' the girl says, directing her gaze now at Brian.

'Oh yes,' Brian smiles but not too widely. He wishes he had flashing white teeth instead of little nicotine-stained ones. The girl's teeth are milk-white and regular.

'I'm on the full-time GCSE course and they said I have to do Communications.'

'That's right,' he says. The girl is toying with a little gold cross, which she pops into her mouth by easing the chain up so that it drapes her chin. Gold studs spangle her ears.

He must talk to her about the course, get her to fill a form in, but he finds he just wants to sit gazing at her without speaking. She looks at a loss as he rallies himself and mutters on about forms and course details and asks her for her name. 'Shelly,' she says. 'Well I'm really called Michele – one "l" – Williamson.'

'Right, Shelly,' he says, 'can you fill this in – just take a seat.' She sits opposite him and he stares at the bone-white line of her parting. Her glossy dark hair lounges about her cheeks. He marvels at the dense darkness of its blue-black depths.

At eight o'clock Janet and Ellie inveigle him into a visit to the pub. 'We need some reinforcement after a day like we've had,' Janet tells him, and he finds himself being swept along and ends up wedged between the thighs of both women in the Queens pub.

'You don't take enough care of yourself, Bri.' Janet sups a half of lager and mummies him. Janet doesn't lose things or make mistakes. She is somebody who has a proper grip on life. He recognises this whilst floating out on a riverboat with the young girl from the afternoon's enrolment session.

Shelly, he subsequently discovers, does not know how to spell, nor can she construct a basic business letter or write a memo. The simplest things seem impossible for her. Whilst he is explaining them to her, she gazes into his face, her shiny lips slightly parted, so that he forgets what he is saying in the wonder of her full, red-lipsticked mouth.

'What are you hoping to do?' he asks her one day after an intense struggle to explain some punctuation rules.

'Oh, I don't know.' She gives a helpless little smile. 'I just want to be famous.'

'Yes,' he says, 'but what else?'

She smiles at him in incomprehension and gives a little giggle. 'Well, I expect I'll end up in a shop.'

'I see. Now can you try, Shelly, to write capital "I" when you mean yourself?'

'But I always do it small.' She gives another helpless giggle. He almost admires her anarchic use of the full stop.

When he sits at home marking the class coursework, he saves Shelly's to the end and then stares at the big curly letters which are so large they fill the entire line and even hit the line above, there being no appreciable difference in size between upper- and lower-case letters. Somehow the handwriting captures Shelly's very essence – it *is* Shelly. As he concentrates on it, it conjures her up.

He writes patient notes at the end of her work, sometimes covering half an A4 page, and Shelly says, 'Brian, I can't understand your writing.' So of course he has to sit beside her and explain. Whilst he is demonstrating something, she always twiddles her hair round a finger or sucks her gold cross, activities which he finds madly distracting.

One evening on his way to the library to borrow some CDs from the music section, he passes a nightclub to which a bevy of young girls are headed. They all have long pale gleaming legs and bare arms although frost sparkles on the pavements. As they walk their hair jigs and their pert little bottoms vibrate. In the middle of them is Shelly in a scarlet sheath. Suddenly a crazy mix of scents engulfs the street. Turning on the steps of the nightclub Shelly spots him and jiggles her fingers at him. The other girls swivel round too and shout, 'Hiya', and burst out into eldritch wolf whistling and giggles before being caught up by a group of young men in white shirts who follow them into the pumping sound.

As Brian enters the library, his cheeks burn.

At the beginning of the summer term all the students' coursework has to be prepared for external moderation. Brian is vaguely aware of Janet and Ellie flapping about and feels pleasantly relaxed because fellow lecturers, closeted in meetings, leave the workrooms untroubled by the noise of their gossiping.

'Bri, have you got the coursework ready from your groups?' Janet enquires after he has spent a morning dibbing into a bag of Thornton's Continental chocolates and catching up on a bit of marking whilst doing the *Guardian* quick crossword.

'What?'

'Coursework, you know, the moderator's in next week.'

'Oh, right.'

There follows forty-eight hours of Brian scrabbling through piles of paperwork to reach the deadline, and by the time the two suited figures appear with their executive cases, he feels quite confident that all is well. However the following morning he is summoned to the Head of Faculty's office.

'Brian, do sit down.' She surveys him across the desk. She always wears a sharp black suit and a long skirt. 'Now, Brian,

I've just had the moderator's report. He is concerned at the standard of your marking and particularly with regard to the coursework of one student, Michele Williamson.'

Brian's hands feel clammy and his cheeks flame. 'Her work,' the voice continues, 'does not merit a pass. What on earth came over you? Well, just look at this!' She pushes Shelly's unpunctuated coursework across at Brian. True, it does in appearance resemble pages from *Finnegans Wake* but he has found himself in thrall to these lower-case 'i's' and the idiosyncratic use of full stops. Shelly seems to stand smiling at him, sucking her cross and twiddling her hair. He has nothing to say and stares at the floor not listening to the Head's diatribe.

Later there are rumblings about suspension for incompetence. Students cannot be at the mercy of people like Brian.

On the last day of the session when Shelly and her group leave, Brian in a deep gloom goes for a drink with Janet and other lecturers. Somehow he and Janet finish the day at his house in bed.

'You just need organising, Bri,' Janet tells him, surveying the dusty clutter of angels and angelic children, Victorian ewers and basins, decorated chamberpots and epergnes which gives the room a curious cavelike aura.

By the time Brian is once more sitting in the hall beside Janet at the start of a new academic year, he is now sharing her Brie and watercress sandwiches and planning on buying her the slender scarlet sheath dress he has glimpsed in a boutique near the College – though what he has not considered is the fact that Janet with her jellying arms and heavy thighs could never squeeze into such a garment …

Open Day

As they step through the swing doors, Jim half glimpses a woman in a black suit striding away down the corridor and he is jolted into the past. Those legs wore jeans and a T-shirt peeped from a jacket. Tendrils of hennaed hair frothed to her shoulders. She fumed and squawked and knew how to irritate, drive you to throttling point. Viv – it has got to be Viv.

Jim stands in the hall beside his son, Sam. The clock still faces you as you enter. That clock is the one 'Daddy' Bently pointed at when you tried to dismiss your apprentices five minutes early and creep out of the building yourself. He lay in wait, and before his finger you were reduced from adult status to that of a jibbering schoolkid. The staircase scrolls up two floors just like in old times – but not quite. Already as they approached the building, he noticed the wire mesh has been removed from the windows. The bricks are no longer smutted but have returned to their original pale biscuit colour. The stalag atmosphere has vanished.

'This it then?' Sam mutters.

'Of course it is.' Jim tries to come on with some bounce.

'It's old.'

A suited woman drenches them with a smile. 'Open evening – yes? Like to take one of these and just go through those doors. Room G24 – all right? You can't miss it.'

'Come on, Dad.'

Jim wants to look about. Sam slouches towards the doors, head tortoising from his baseball cap. He didn't want to come; he doesn't want to do anything except protest, but now that he's here, he wants it over with fast.

Once in the corridor Jim glances round. Gone are the flagged walkways and the workshops with their concrete floors. The line of sinks has vanished. The ceilings have been lowered. Carpet squares create wide tweedy spaces. Computers squat on working surfaces. The awful chill has been replaced by a double-glazed, sealed-in mugginess.

They pause in the doorway of a room where people sit at tables whilst prospective students and their parents gather round them.

Jim heads, with Sam trailing in the rear, for a table labelled A-Levels, and presiding behind it Jim sees Viv, who darts a look at him.

'Hi, Jim,' she says. She obviously isn't going to pretend she doesn't know him. He notices Sam's surprise.

'Great to see you,' he says.

'This your son?'

'Yes – Sam. He wants to do some A-Levels.' Sam glowers. Jim struggles with embarrassment and a certain pleasure, because in a way he is glad to see her.

Viv introduces herself to Sam. 'Sit down both of you – your Dad worked here with me many moons ago.'

'Oh, nice one.' Sam ducks his head and peers at his Nike trainers.

Jim watches her turning through leaflets and focussing her remarks on Sam. She has very small fingers for such a tall woman. He notes that they are ringless. Their tips involve themselves with the papers, so that watching her you get an idea they must contain some esoteric information.

He loses track of what she and Sam are discussing. Twenty-five years ago this place resounded with apprentices. Carps and joiners planed wood and sawed. Blond curls escaped onto the flagged corridors. Somewhere groups welded, eyes protected by goggles, and fumes belched under doors, a small portion channelled away by the gigantic metal chimney outside in the yard behind the building. This puffed fumes up into the sky – well the ones that didn't reach the corridors first.

Upstairs drama raged in General Studies lessons. Each class must be entertained or the thirty or so lads, direct from building sites or shipbuilders' yards – the apprentice gas fitters, plumbers, carpenters, joiners and motor-vehicle mechanics – took the lesson apart. (What use is General Studies? I didn't come here to learn about all this political stuff – who cares?) You learned never to reply to the opening gambit: What use is fucking General Studies?

Only the favoured lecturers got exam classes. Sensitive souls were driven mad; some resigned; one threw himself on the railway track to be ploughed down by the seven p.m. London Intercity.

He stares round at the teenagers and the lecturers doling out advice. Nowadays all the staff apparently wear suits – men in collars and ties, and they have short hair. No more jeans, cheese-cloth shirts, hair trailing on shoulders and down backs, and women in Indian Imports dresses. Gone is the chink of sandalwood beads. Towards the end of the summer term such as this the sniping started. Registers must be totalled up. Viv, of course, didn't do hers. Can't do percentages. She tried to face him down – as though not being able to do percentages were not a failing. She wanted him to total her registers and write in percentage attendances, but she wouldn't ask – oh no. Viv would never ask for something. She merely slapped the registers at him.

The battle of the classroom took place in the summer term too. She commandeered his room to show some film or other.

Her eyes opened very wide at him – pale turquoise glass shone into his face: 'It's all arranged – has been for ages. I sent you a memo.'

He had a film lined up about gruesome industrial accidents for his shipbuilders, those hefty Vikings soon to become extinct, although they didn't know it at the time. The showing of films was a pacifier, a way of soothing the savage hordes. He became incensed at the thought of losing two hours' peace. Whilst the figures moved across the screen, the Vikings sat still in the brown gloom, attention focussed for once, and he could relax and need not brace himself for a renewed onslaught.

They confronted each other in the classroom doorway. She had already taken possession and her rows of hairdressing apprentices sat preening and giggling and twisting round to see his Viking mob, who jammed the corridor trying to peer at the girls.

'I can't understand why you're making such a performance about it,' she said, giving him that condescending turquoise stare.

'No, you wouldn't.'

He wanted to shout obscenities, pulverise her, and behind his back the mob tried to egg him on and made suggestive sucking noises.

'We'll see about this,' he hissed through gritted teeth.

But he had to withdraw, step back, take the group to another classroom and struggle through two breathless hours, with pellets zinging about the air and boots kicking desks and yawns and natterings as he tried to stir up a debate on 'Capital Punishment should be re-introduced.' The problem with such a topic was that nobody would speak against the motion. Nor did he feel like doing so after grappling with them all that afternoon.

He saw her in the corridor later, loping along, shoulders hunched, hair fizzing, face a relaxed cream oval. She had enjoyed two hours of comfort, whilst he frazzled and sweated and longed for a mug of coffee and a fag.

Another rerun of that afternoon followed the next week. She thought the room was now hers. He realised that he must occupy it first, and by marshalling the shipbuilders earlier than usual, he succeeded. When she opened the door, expecting to find an empty room, her gaze ricocheted against his. The pink whooshed into her cheeks and her eyes sparkled. Behind her he could hear the squawking of her hairdressing apprentices, excited by the near presence of the hulking youths.

'You know I've booked it,' she said.

'No you haven't – it's my room anyway.'

'We don't own rooms.'

'I am timetabled to be in here.'

'Nonsense!'

'Go on, tell her – you give her one, Jimo.' Around him apprentices cheered him on. He hated her, her arrogance – she thought she was Simone de Beauvoir or Kate Millet or some other feminist icon and that meant squashing men, castrating them.

She didn't wear deodorant and she let the hair bush in her armpits and she ate raw garlic and went braless so that you saw her nipples poking up under her T-shirts and she didn't care that her breasts were tiny like hard fruits. Other lecturers wore lipstick and eye make-up – not she – and yet about her there was something annoyingly sexy. It made him cringe.

'Well are you moving out then?'

Pause

'Or do I report you?'

Report. That was rich – that was totally rich. She couldn't have said anything worse. Never, never would he give up the room now. He turned and smiled full in her face, and closed the door. The shipbuilders cheered and shook their fists in the air. After some consultation in the corridor outside, she and her hairdressers retreated.

The following day he was summoned to the Head of Department's office. What did he think he was doing – Ms Bates had as much right to use the projection room as he etc. He fumed and wanted to strangle her.

She gave him a little smile as she led her group into the room on the next occasion.

'You given in to her then?' the shipbuilders wanted to know. He thought he detected scorn in their voices.

Timetabling was in progress. Nobody of course wanted Plumbers III General Studs last thing Friday afternoon. He smiled noticing V Bates occupying that square on the master timetable. An hour later when he picked up his personal timetable from his pigeonhole, he discovered his name marked in that Friday afternoon slot.

'Bitch!' he bellowed. 'Cow!'

Other workroom members raised their heads from frenzied register-totalling or the clearing out of drawers, and stared at him.

He came across her in the empty student commonroom smoking a roll-up and stirring sugar into a mug of tea whilst reading the Women's Page of the *Guardian*.

'You cow,' he snarled.

She looked up unconcerned and fixed those turquoise eyes on him. 'What?'

'You did it, didn't you?'

'What are you on about?'

'I'll sling you through that fucking window,' he yelled.

She came on all prim and he shook with rage, because she seemed so unassailable.

'For God's sake, Jim, it's your testosterone.'

'Don't – if you think you've landed me with that Friday afternoon, you're in for a surprise.'

The matter of Plumbers III passed back and forth like some ticking time bomb, which each recipient tossed to the next victim in the hope of escaping the ultimate explosion. By the next afternoon she had acquired it again. She stopped him in the workroom.

'I hope you're satisfied now.'

His answer was a smile.

'You slimy little prat – you ball-less wonder.'

'Thanks for that.'

He drove home feeling oddly put out. Something about the shape of her tiny breasts and her thick pouty lips disarmed him.

At the end-of-session 'do' he noticed Glenn, a new chap, had his hand on her bottom. The fingers pressed and splayed themselves.

He embarrasses himself now in remembering how he caused Glenn to spill a pint over his cream suit, and this later resulted in them slipping and sliding as they slugged it out in a very amateurish manner with a lot of puffing and lunging.

By this time he and Jane had been married for five years, and division-of-labour struggles had already started. He was so obsessed with the battles at college and how to outwit Viv that he was shocked when Jane asked him to leave.

Not many months after that he started applying for new jobs and then he was leaving. Another end-of-term party and Viv actually bought him a drink.

'So you're away,' she said.

'Yes, pastures new.'

The Glenn affair was obviously over because they weren't bothering with each other. Anyway rumour broadcast that she went through men like a wire through cheese. She was independent and there was no nonsense about 'love'.

At some point when she sat back, stared into his face and said, 'You know, I'll quite miss you, you little prat' – it took his breath away, as did the smile she shone on him. He'd been dallying in a very promiscuous phase since his divorce, but then,

meeting those turquoise eyes, he paused. Elation seized him
and he just wanted to hold her. The moment seemed to widen
out and deepen as their eyes met, but then he plunged into
despair, because she had been the focus in him of so much
emotion, and now he wouldn't in all probability ever see her
again. And of course he hasn't until now, though he has heard
about her through gossip from ex-colleagues. She didn't take
up with anyone but one day she announced she was pregnant.
Nobody knew who the father might be, and she has reared her
daughter single-handed. Even that intrigues him.

'I'm just suggesting Sam go to talk with the Philosophy lecturer over there.' She is addressing him and he makes an effort
to concentrate.

'Fine.'

Sam has departed to a table across the room, leaving them
alone together.

'You've been here ever since?' he says.

'Sure – why not – you can run but you always end up back at
the same place anyway.'

'Yes,' he says, 'I suppose so.'

'He seems a bright lad.'

'Sam? Yes – he's been very difficult lately though – been
expelled from his school.'

'I gathered.'

'He told you?'

'Oh yes.'

'Well, at least you've got him to talk. Kids!' He gives a groan
and smiles.

'How many?'

'Three.'

'You've been busy.'

'What about you?'

'A daughter.'

She bears her age well, he thinks, even the pronounced hunching of her shoulders is attractive, because it links her to her past. In one way she's updated – she's gone with the new flooring and the lowered ceilings; she's all suits and blouses – but he can still glimpse intriguing traces of the past.

'Would you dare to have a drink with me – like next week?' he says, as he feels his face growing hot. 'I think we owe it to the projection room.'

She gives a grin that exposes several gaps in her molars and her eyes crinkle up. 'Well, why not.'

He wants to sing as he leaves the building with Sam, who babbles on about his proposed course. Outside Jim turns round to stare up once more at the biscuit-coloured facade of the Tech College building and he sucks in a deep breath.

'Come on Dad, come on,' Sam chivvies.

The Brothers

It's a day of thin high cloud, burnished trees and late warmth as Tony leaves his office, crosses to M&S, buys a cheese-and-pickle sandwich and a carton of pure orange and makes for the park. Tab-end days like this stir his nostalgia; they hint at scouring-sweet moments, like the itchy spot you must scratch to the point of pleasure that turns to agony.

He goes down the steps into the grassy area, which is littered with young kids from the college on lunch-hour break. A blond girl stretches on her back and above her a lad poises himself. Tony catches the dense aura of desire. Sex is everywhere. It oozes from wooden benches where kids pat banter back and forth; it is in the four inches of midriff peeping as a girl rolls on the grass or squats exposing the thin line of a thong and the plumping of her buttocks; it is in the waggle of a passing girl's bum under tight black trousers. Sun spangles flesh. Girls' scent and lads' body sprays tickle his nostrils.

The council workers have started to prune the roses but a few blossoms still remain, their petals pale and waxy. Mallards snooze under the trees and the paths are splattered with birdlime.

The sight of all these kids in the still warmth, nibbling, sucking, letting hands slide down jeans-clad thighs, won't let him escape Adele. Twelve years separate him from those times when they were sixteen. Adele bleached her bob even then and always wore white face powder. His Gran said, 'My goodness, that girl looks like death on the road.' Adele had to lie on the floor to pull her jeans on.

He's been away from here for five years, and coming back

now to work in the city everything seems achingly the same only smaller. This time of year hurts because the old crackling excitement lurks round every corner. Late September, early October, is when people you've forgotten suddenly jump out of the woodwork. Kids start new courses, new years, the exodus to university gets underway. It has all happened to him before.

He chooses a seat in a recess facing one of the ornamental ponds. The flags rustle in a faint breeze and a mallard paddles its orange feet, stirring the ripples. Under the seat several discarded lager cans roll and lazy wasps buzz. As he unpeels the plastic wrapping on the sandwiches, he chances to look up and glances straight at a shortish man whose auburn hair resembles hedgehog spines. His cheeks are spiny too.

Tony takes him in at a glance: black cotton polo neck, black very worn jeans, battered Doc Martens and of course the big gold earring. Irritation and embarrassment battle for mastery. He finds his cheeks growing hot. Will he pass without a word? Shall he pretend he hasn't seen him? The pathway is too narrow for that. Tony, sitting there in his navy office suit, white shirt and navy tie, has the urge to push the other man into the pond and watch him gurgle with surprise and indignation as he flounders amongst the twining lily roots and the dead beer bottles and sharp stones. The bottom of the pond will be lined with thick black stinking silt and the stench will always cling to those jeans and that polo neck no matter how he washes them. But of course he's not the man to unleash violence.

The past, though, is strewn with dubious moments, like the time when Tony found his favourite Star Wars figure broken, or his Walkman missing; still later his best white shirt minus two buttons and with a grease mark down the front which nothing would remove. The ruination of the Star Wars figure led to Tony battering him until his nose bled.

'Hi,' the spiny-headed one says.

'Hello.' Tony tries to smile at his brother with whom he hasn't spoken for five years. He wishes his cheeks would cool down.

'Fancy bumping into you,' Martin says, 'Mum told me you'd come back.'

'Yes,' Tony says, dodging his brother's eyes, which are toffee-coloured and sincere. If only they wouldn't blaze with such openness. Things don't change. Martin has always been the same, smiling good-naturedly whilst he casually tramples over you without realising it. Or does he really know what havoc he wreaks? 'I'm just having a bite to eat,' Tony announces and concentrates on his sandwich, hoping that this will cause Martin to back off.

'Oh right.'

Instead Martin sits down beside him. There are two cheese-and-pickle sandwiches in the packet, now he will have to offer Martin one and he doesn't want to; he'll feel hungry if he only eats one. Irritation bubbles. Martin invariably puts him in the position where he, Tony, must sacrifice with a smile on his face, whilst Martin graciously accepts though behaving as though he is doing Tony a favour.

'Have a sandwich,' Tony says, proffering the packet.

'Ta.' Martin nips up a sandwich and chomps away with enthusiasm, the odd crumb bowling away to be flown after by a pigeon. Tony takes small bites and wipes a tissue fastidiously across his lips periodically, careful not to drop crumbs on his suit. He darts a sideways glance at his brother's clothes. Martin's sweatshirts were always stained with food or stippled with roll-up ash with tiny holes here and there. For years he wore a leather jacket from which a pocket dangled.

A lager haze rises from the cans under the seat. This must definitely be the winos pitch.

'So how've you been?' Martin opens. He has already gobbled down his sandwich. Tony has another half of his to go. His irritation deepens. He could throttle Martin without any problem and he's sure he would feel better if he did.

People who say that virtue is rewarded are idiots. Between the two of them it is always Martin the loser who reaps the rewards. Off he went to art college. He was only going to be the second Picasso. It was black talons, long dyed black hair, thousands of tinkling bracelets, and wherever he went he sounded like those security systems that ring bells when you enter a place. And of course there was the fake diamond nose jewel. After partying solidly for two years he was slung out by the college authorities. Did the parents castigate him? Not on your life. It was, 'Well, Martin, oh well, that's just Martin.' Hands flapped with helpless acceptance and more cash was handed across, because Martin was like that. He just had to smile and mumble apologies and he was home and dry.

Then there'd be the girls ringing up Mother, hoping they could enlist her assistance, because Martin had dropped them; they were always very pretty. They had to be.

Tony realises that his brother is still waiting for his reply. 'All right,' he says, keeping his eyes focussed on the last bite of his sandwich.

'Looking very dapper as usual – smart suit and all.'

Is Martin laughing at him? Tony chances a quick look at his smiling ginger face. It's the mug of a ginger tom. He has never liked cats; they leave hair all over and dig up the borders, where they shit, and spread fleas about.

'Well, can't go round looking like a slob.'

'Yes, look the part, the wealthy accountant.' Martin says it as though it's an insult, but he continues to smile. Tony wants to smash the smile off his face.

'What about you then?' Tony turns the interrogation on Martin, the junior brother, the one who should be questioned.

'Well this and that. The band folded. I'm doing some DJ-ing, trying to get a foot in there.'

'Oh, you aren't looking for work then?'

'Not exactly. Just been to sign on as a matter of fact. It's my signing-on day.'

'No job prospects then?' These aren't the questions Tony wants to ask, but he doesn't know how to frame the big question; the one that has eaten away at him, been at the back of his every waking thought for the last five years. He has never been able to throw hurts off easily; with him they fester. There was the time at school when his best mate, Jim Frazer, ganged up against him. 'Oh, it was only a joke, Ton, only a joke.' But Tony has never forgotten it and from that moment he no longer considered Frazer to be a friend. The Frazer incident, though, is nothing compared with the thing between him and Martin.

'You glad to be back?'

'Haven't really thought about it.' Tony picks non-existent pieces of fluff off his suit jacket and stares at the mallards pecking about in the reeds. 'Things don't seem to change very much here.'

'Well I'm about ready for a big change.'

Tony is shocked to hear a note of iron come into his brother's voice. The usual joky, skidding-along-the-surface slur of words has slipped away. Martin doesn't look at him now, he gazes away down the gardens, down the alley of flowering almond trees, whose foliage has turned copper and gold. Ochre leaves trickle down.

'Like what?' Tony says, feeling a tightness in his chest. He wants to peel the leaves from his shiny black lace-ups but can't seem to move for fear lest the moment shift direction. Anxiety churns in his stomach. He couldn't care less about Martin's big change. But of course he could.

'Think I might go abroad.'

'What would you do there?'

'DJ-ing if poss.'

'Right.'

'There's no point in hanging around here.'

Tony forgets the leaves on his shoes and the irritation of sharing his sandwiches as another thought strikes him. Anger makes his body molten with heat. Is it possible that the little prat has left her, just like he did all the rest?

He'd had suspicions. Oh yes, there were hints: Adele's bursts of vivacity around Martin; hot glances; his hand on her buttocks. Was a pat something more? Men don't pat women's buttocks unless they're lovers. He is back, plunged into the maelstrom of those days and weeks, which led up to the evening Adele made her announcement.

'Ton, I've got something to tell you. I'm sorry about it, but me and you aren't really suited.'

He badgered her for the real reason. People didn't suddenly become 'unsuited'. In the end she let him have it. 'I'm in love with Martin and we're moving in together.' Just like that. A slap across the face.

He relives that rush of adrenaline and the hate. It grew into a physical pain. He has never had it out with Martin. There has just been silence between them, because Tony realises now he has always known that he is capable of killing Martin. This hate, stored for an age, has been suppressed too long.

If he hadn't loved Adele it would have been different. He still remembers the satin of her skin; the butterfly tattoo on her left buttock; the mole by the corner of her mouth; curly feet in clumpy sling-backs and shiny scarlet toenails and the thin gold chain round her ankle – overblown, clichéd things, so much titillation; but then an honesty and her laughter. She liked fun and couldn't get enough of it. 'Oh hell, Ton, don't be so stuffy – loosen up, get your tie off. Enjoy life a bit.' At that time he didn't know what she meant.

'All right,' he says, fired up so that he turns on his brother, 'so what's happened to Adele? I expect you dumped her as well, did you?'

If Martin says yes, Tony knows he will batter him into the pond. The day whirls. The stench of lager sticks in his nostril and he listens to the pounding of his blood. He used to play that picture back and back: Martin and Adele naked, sprawled on the sheets. He howled with pain at it; the knowledge that they both shared all these private things. For days he would catch himself pondering on whether Adele noticed any difference between them. Could she have told Tony from Martin in the night, or was all flesh the same? His curiosity knew no bounds. Is he better at it than me? What has he got that I haven't? These sorts of questions. But people don't admit things like this ever.

Martin doesn't seem to be aware of him and looks curiously lumpish, staring now at the pond.

'Well?'

'If you want to know,' he barks, 'she left me. She's got some git with a lot of cash.'

Tony, thrown of balance, doesn't know what to say.

For no apparent reason he is back with Martin in their grandfather's greenhouse. Granddad kept the greenhouse warm in winter by using an old coke boiler. To raddle the ash out he used a very thin poker with a bent end. The poker always fascinated Tony. He liked to see it glowing red. On that day he heated it by plunging it into the heart of the boiler and fetched it out to brandish at Martin. Whether or not he meant to brand him with it, Tony doesn't know, but he caught his brother just below the eye. Martin bellowed with agony and raced away, hands clutched to his face. Tony stared after him, terrified, still holding the poker, which he hurled at the boiler and then took off after Martin.

'You could have blinded him,' his Gran said. 'You should know better.'

Should know better. The staring red burn on the pale flesh turned purplish and yellow and it left a scar, which still shows; scars, Tony realises, contain important personal histories.

Martin turns to look at Tony. 'I suppose you're pleased.'

The blood surges into Tony's face again. He has to gaze at the scar beneath Martin's eye.

'I know I shouldn't have taken her from you.'

Tony is shocked to hear his own voice saying, 'Martin, nobody can take someone from another person. Adele went because she didn't love me. Listen, I've got to get back to work now. Let's meet tonight. Come round to my place.'

As Tony leaves Martin, crossing by the ponds to the steps leading onto the pavement, it is as though a weight has been lifted from him.

The Jacket

They are about to sit down at the kitchen table to eat 'Nasi Boring', which is Nick's name for his mother's rice and leftover chicken concoction. He likes strong-flavoured, oily, fatty things but his mother, always intent on saving the household from coronary heart disease and strokes, dishes up bland meals lacking zing. Nick eyes the stainless steel pot with dissatisfaction.

'Don't start!' his mother says, big-eyeing him with a twitch of laughter in her lips.

'Nasi Boring again,' he pronounces.

'We haven't had it for three weeks.'

'Counting, are you?' They grin at each other. A draught percolates under the kitchen door.

'Dad's here,' Nick registers. He's feeling on edge, his insides jitter like bundles of wrongly connected electric wiring. Tomorrow is the job interview. Ever since he opened the envelope, he has traced this uneasiness in his middle.

'No, don't wait. Don't think of it!' his Dad gusts in smiling. 'Don't wait, wouldn't want you to.'

His father's mouth is a letterbox slit and the corners jimp in a grin which exposes his odd assortment of Stonehenge teeth.

'It's Nasi Boring,' Nick repeats.

'Oh, good,' his Dad says and starts to eat. Nick eyes his Dad's grease-stained, cracked-leather hands. With Dad there is no nonsense about washing hands before meals; hungry, then he just gets stuck in.

'Job interview,' Nick groans.

'Missing you already,' his Dad says, shovelling up his Nasi

Goreng at a good speed with his fork and twinkling at Nick in the moments when he raises his eyes from his plate.

'It's all right for you,' Nick chunters, belching.

'Of course – on roofs, under floors.'

'I bet you've been frozen today,' Nick's mother says.

'Not too bad.'

Nick wonders why his Dad never seems to feel the cold. It's no use asking him what the weather's like because he invariably classes it as 'mild'. Nick hates freezing temperatures. 'Don't know what to put on for this stupid interview,' he whines. 'I haven't got anything.'

'Well, lad, I've got something for you.'

There is a short silence punctuated only by forks scraping on plates and the steam-engine hiss of the central-heating boiler. Nick thinks this over. His Dad is like nobody else's dad, something he realised long ago. Whereas Nick always has his antennae a-quiver as they sense how the outside world is reacting to him, his Dad appears to plunge on regardless of what other people think.

When he was little, Nick would be hurrying to keep up with his Dad's hectic pace as he went at a shamble in his burst plimsoles, saggy jackets swinging in rhythm, hair fanning out like a mad dandelion clock in the breeze. At such times Nick's eyes in metal-detector fashion were glued to the pavement and he stumbled along over his toes, because Dad had given out the instruction: Eyes down for yens, kopecks and pound coins.

This of course was quite interesting when he was four, but by the time he reached fourteen Nick blushed with embarrassment to see his Dad in public stooping to retrieve 2p from the gutter, after which he polished it on his jeans with evident satisfaction and finally flourished it as a great find.

Around this time, too, there were occasions with Dad, out at the cinema or in town, when Nick glimpsed a posse of kids from his class. Mortified, he learned to pretend he was on his own so that the lads wouldn't realise this character with the tough, battered face, vagrant's clothing and outlandish behaviour was anything to do with him. Their dads wore suits or expensive casual clothing and behaved as fathers should in a restrained abstracted fashion.

Odd types always made for his Dad. That too has happened for years and seems inevitable. He is the one whom tramps accost and beggars implore. Any visit to town is punctuated by Dad raking his pockets for pound coins, which he doles out to desperate cases squatting on the pavement and young girls with dogs and boys playing flutes. Once a shabby unlikely character appeared at the door and Dad let him in. He sat in the kitchen and was offered tea and a sandwich by Nick's mother. 'Na, can't eat that stuff,' the man spat, eyeing the brown bread with disgust, 'have ye no any white?' He took four spoons of sugar in his tea and rattled the spoon in the mug fit to smash it. Finally he asked Dad to run off with him to Scotland. Dad said, 'Sorry my friend,' and encouraged the man to drift off.

By this time Dad is wiping the back of his hand across his mouth and quaffing long on his mug of tea.

'Want to see what I've got you, lad?'

Nick nods, despite deep reservations. He meets his mother's eye but she merely looks mystified. His father leaves the kitchen and returns a couple of minutes later with two jackets, both on coat hangers and shrouded in pieces of plastic.

'Designer jackets,' his father says.

'Oh, er, right.'

His father unveils one of them, as though he were a sculptor revealing a masterpiece to the public eye.

The jacket is black, zip-fronted and of a soft slithery material. It is emblazoned with an intricate logo, which Nick does not recognise. He does not wear clothes like this and he cannot bear the idea of putting on such a jacket. It has a dodgy knowy look.

'There was this chap in a left-hand-drive car – he pulls up, doesn't he, calls me over – "Now then," he says, "what about some designer jackets? I need some petrol money." He said he was Italian. Wanted £60. I said no chance.'

His Dad does not disclose the amount paid. Nick listens carefully but his Dad never actually spells it out.

'Said I could have more – jackets for my relatives, friends.'

Nick can imagine the scene – some long black car and the driver, black hair slicked back with gel, a fast talker in a sharp suit, a really wide guy. Nick can also see that the sleeves are way too short for him. He is tall and long-limbed. He finds himself grinning and wants to make a facetious remark but his Dad's exuberant expression halts him.

'Come on then, try it on!'

'But Dad you could get done for receiving.'

'I was just buying a couple of jackets.'

'But off some dodgy bloke.'

'Na,' his Dad dismisses objections with a swift wave of the hand. 'Well, try it on then.'

Laughing, unable to keep the mockery out of his tone, Nick picks at the plastic. 'I'll feel a right lunatic in this.' But nevertheless he slides his arms into the garment. His wrists protrude several inches beyond the cuffs as he suspected they would.

'It's a grand fit – there you are,' his Dad concludes, 'bound to get the job with that on.'

'I don't think.'

'Well, aren't you pleased?'

'Yer, yer, ecstatic!'

The next day he leaves the house wearing the jacket. He keeps his hands in his pockets so that the shortness of the sleeves will be less obvious.

It's another freezing day with an east wind blasting in his

face and striking through the silky material. Before he reaches the office block where the interview is to be held, he removes the jacket and bundles it under his arm. Frozen in his white shirt, he steps into the lift, which zooms up to the third floor. Suited forms stride past him. It's a relief to be in the warm corridors.

A girl in the reception tinkles at him and stares at his white shirt. Mr Smithson wouldn't be long, would he like to take a seat. Well, he wouldn't but he does.

Mr Smithson, when he does summon Nick into his office after fifteen minutes, is another of the suited types, and very superior. He chases bits in his nails with a paperclip whilst speaking. At some point his eyes blaze full into Nick's. 'You must be a warm-blooded sort – it's freezing out there isn't it?'

'Yes, well, I don't seem to feel the cold,' Nick says, thinking of his Dad.

'Start Monday with a six-month trial period,' the boss-man, Smithson, says eventually. Nick gives a polite smile, thanks him and tries to appear animated, then it's back out into the street.

Once well away from the six-storey office block, he puts on the jacket. He's meeting Dad in town for lunch. Dad is good for lunches. He makes a celebration of them. From far away he can see the familiar figure waiting.

'Well?'

'Got it – six-month trial.'

'Well done, lad!' His Dad gives him a heavy pat on the shoulder. 'See, I told you the jacket would help.'

'Yer, yer, that's right.'

Crossing the pedestrian precinct on their way to the café his Dad likes, they run into a skirmish. One of the pasty lads who sits on the pavement and begs with a plastic cup in front of him is fighting a big chap in a navy suit. Nobody seems to be taking any notice.

Before Nick has realised it, his Dad has run forward and seized the arm of the big chap and is trying to drag him off the boy. In no time two more big heavies, also in navy suits, belt up and grab the lad, whilst his Dad and the first man end up nose to nose.

The lad now has handcuffs on his wrists. A police van shoots onto the precinct and the lad is pushed in. The big man flashes a card at Dad, who, totally unimpressed, scowls at him but backs off.

The scene has all happened in a blink and yet in that time Nick has gone from surprise to fear to admiration, and when his Dad stoops later to retrieve a 5p coin, he feels warmed by the familiar gesture.

Monday sees him entering the six-storey office block in his new designer jacket and feeling quite proud of it.

Caps

Caps in Tom's family are potent symbols and not merely something worn on the head. Of course Tom's relationship with his cap is quite different from that of his grandfather.

Grandfather Frank was ninety when Tom first saw him sprottling in an armchair at his aunt's house. Tom, being only three at the time, didn't understand the intricacies of the cap issue.

Marigold photographs taken in 1914 when Frank was nineteen show him bareheaded with black hair parted down the centre falling in curtains about his face. His friends have caps jammed down on their foreheads. Frank was a conscientious objector in the First World War and in his photograph collection are pictures of fellow C.O.s, often men from middle-class families. They have trilbies perched on their heads – no flat caps here.

Frank, who started his working life as a messenger boy in a steel works, learnt French, German and Spanish during three years in Dartmoor Prison as a C.O. This, upon his release, placed him as a translator of letters in the foreign department of a steel works, in the non-cap-wearing class. From then on he sported a soft brown trilby. By this time, too, he had lost his thick black hair, the loss of which from his late twenties onwards gave the misleading impression of his being a tonsured monk.

But caps, although shunned earlier in Frank's life, cosied their way in later. Tom's father, Rob, would see his father on Saturday mornings, flat cap slotted on his baldpate, shambling off to his greenhouse at the bottom of the garden. He would be joined there by Old Archie, a dedicated cap-wearer. Old Archie had been gardener to a duke but in retirement he lived in a back-to-back with an asphalted yard and no garden, so he took refuge in the family garden. He potted up chrysanthemums and geranium cuttings and pricked out seedlings in the greenhouse, whilst his asthma snorted and whined. Only very occasionally did he remove his cap and that would be to swipe at the Baskervilles, two sausage dogs, who snouted under the greenhouse benches. 'Getcha!' he growled making mock lunges and scything at them with his cap.

After mornings spent in the greenhouse or repairing the Great Wall of China, the perimeter wall enclosing the garden, Frank executed various domestic manoeuvres with the joint spitting in the oven of the kitchen coke stove, in time for the appearance of his wife from work at two p.m.

Following the meal Frank was to be found curled up, snoozing on the front-room floor, cap still on his head and an old coat thrown over him. An hour or so later he creaked up, blinked, negotiated his glasses back on his face and rose, yawning, ready for another spell out of doors.

Caps were for him in middle and old age an intimate comfort but nevertheless objects not to be worn outside the Wall of China. In the world beyond he continued to wear one of his wavy-brimmed trilbies.

Rob, Frank's son and Tom's father, has never worn any kind of cap – that is with one exception. He is a builder and sometimes for shinning along roofs in a downpour he will pull on a waterproof cap, a curious double-decker creation which gives him a jaunty air and makes Tom laugh. It doesn't resemble the tweedy caps Tom sees old chaps wearing in the street. They seem much flatter, rather like the huge toadstools you may find growing in damp places. Men in those caps have a certain routine with them. When not in use, the caps are folded up into Cornish pasties and slipped into the owners' pockets.

Now Rob's waterproof cap doesn't resemble Tom's cap in any way. Tom's caps are another story. It all started when Tom was fifteen. First you only saw them in films or on telly and then, wham, they had arrived: American baseball caps! The advent of the cap in Tom's life coincided with his first stirrings of rebellion and these seemed to focus on the cap.

A lad he had known for most of his life, Jason, the son of a university lecturer and a year older than himself, wore a cap. He also smoked spliffs. Gatherings took place in Tom's Dad's allotment hut or Jason's room – Jason's Dad, being very abstracted most of the time and on a higher plane and busy with his girlfriends, didn't really notice what his son happened to be doing.

Tom lusted after Jason's black cap with its thick white tick decorating the front above the neb. Caps sprouted everywhere. They were an essential adjunct to the image which Jason cultivated. You aimed at wafters, Blue Bolt jeans with twenty-two inch bottoms, black or grey hooded tops and THE CAP. You listened to drum and bass, smoked spliffs in a concentrated, intense way, inhaling every last twist of smoke, and you were not going to study or go to university or do anything your parents wanted. And never, never, never were you going to have a job. Work must be avoided at all cost. Everything was ghastly, just one great, ginormous whine. This seemed to coincide too with the rise of Oasis and their hit 'Wonderwall', which Tom played incessantly on his tape deck after a run-in with his father over a cap. His father's attitude was: You don't need a cap – they're ugly – it's just an American gimmick.

In the end his father gave way and took him to the city-centre shopping precinct one Saturday. They zoomed up to the top floor on the escalator and wandered through little units selling Indian frogged velvet jackets, floaty cotton skirts, candles, incense and finally found a store devoted solely to caps. Tom stood entranced, gazing at lines of caps; caps squiggled with hieroglyphs; blue, black, white, scarlet and caramel caps. His Dad is the sort of man who shoots into shops, picks up a single garment and says, 'I'll have this, please,' and catapults out again. Not for him is the pleasant meander or the obsessive focussing. He simply couldn't understand why Tom spent so long staring at the nebs and then feeling their stiffness, studying the logos.

'Well,' he said, 'have you made your mind up?'

'Yer, Dad, just a sec.'

Another wait and then finally, 'Do hurry now – I've only a couple of minutes left on the meter.'

Home they drove with the purchase. Tom wore it to meals; he wore it everywhere except in bed. At school the Maths teacher said, 'I am not having people wearing caps in class. If you insist on bringing caps into school, they will be confiscated.'

That made another addition to the 'I hate school' list. He hated his uniform and his stupid black shoes. It was all too much; everybody was of the same opinion.

Jason suggested a Saturday visit to the shopping precinct, which was where everybody hung out, standing at the rails on the various levels and peering at other kids riding the escalators. They could of course have a smoke.

Off they shuffled together with Gareth, another of Jason's mates. You must cultivate a dragging of the feet in your unfastened Nike or Adidas trainers and your wafters caught the pavements and made a faint slithering sound. You had your cap pulled well down or on back to front, grungy sweaters and sweatshirts dangling and flapping, fingerless gloves picking at hems. Tom felt right, sandwiched between Jason and Gareth, slouching forward as one.

The precinct rumbled with shoppers and tunes. A glass lift jolted up to the top floor. The three lost one another in the onrush of people. Tom was soon surrounded by a gaggle of men in their twenties. They too wore baseball caps. One man even taller than beanpole Tom grabbed the cap from Tom's head. Then they were away, lost in the throng. Tom was stabbed by a sense of loss. His cap, so newly acquired, had been wrested from him. He remembered the blunt, chipped faces of the men and he was scared and angry.

His father, being kind-hearted, bought Tom a replacement cap, but this did nothing to extinguish Tom's smouldering rebellion. The night Tom shaved his head marked the start of all-out war. His father bellowed at him, 'It's ugly … ugly – you look like some escapee from an institution.' He raved on. Tom banged out of the room and made off in the night to a mate's flat – the mate was rebelling too and had been thrown out by his parents.

Weeks passed in a haze of spliff smoke, the thrum of drum and bass and spasmodic school attendances. It was sixth form now and so he could wear his wafters and his cap. He needed the cap to keep the chill from his shaven head – but the cap was the badge of something; it stood for rebellion; it showed people who he was; he wasn't going to be forced into a mould.

Gradually the cohorts began to disappear. Jason was expelled from school; Gareth's lecturer father moved to another university; some lads got jobs. Tom moved back home and there was a jumpy truce. He still shaved his head; he still wore the cap, one of a new generation of caps. Only now everyone seemed to be shaven-headed and becapped.

Then it was away to university. There caps and shaven heads didn't evoke any response – they were commonplace. He stopped shaving his head.

At the time of Tom's graduation, his parents arrived for the ceremony and afterwards they went shopping and his Dad bought him a very expensive scarlet cap, which sported an American designer label. Tom was delighted with it.

On returning home, one afternoon, Tom entered the kitchen to make himself a toasted sandwich and intercepted three youths in baseball caps trying to steal an antique urn and some chimney pots from the back garden. He banged on the window and shook his fist, then unlocked the backdoor to go in pursuit, but hoping they would clear off first. They did.

'What did they look like?' his Dad asked later.

'Pretty rough,' Tom said but omitted to mention the detail of the baseball caps. And somehow after that he preferred to keep his cap collection neatly ranged up on the top of a cupboard where they lent the room a certain decorative interest.

A Question of Identity

Jamie isn't the sort of twenty-one-year-old to have had lots of girlfriends. When his friends started fumbling with girls at fifteen and sixteen, he kept well away. Being narrow-chested, gangly and taking size eleven shoes meant that he puffed his guts out and fell over his own feet in sprints and stumbled in last to slow handclaps. In football his feet had a mind of their own and rarely made contact with the ball, nor could he catch at cricket.

Girls seemed to like sporty boys with muscles and casual assurance. Jamie never felt he could approach them. Anyway, the girls he fancied at school were invariably the pansy-faced ones with long straight legs, pert bottoms and blouses always tucked so neatly into waistbands. They mesmerised with their sophistication and just-rightness, but they were claimed by the broad-shouldered, hard-bodied types who seemed sure of their place in the world and moved through the day with certainty stamped on their faces.

Of course that has all changed, fallen away, although the bruises and gashes of childhood have still left scars. He catches himself remembering as he walks into town with Laura.

Four years away at university with only short periods back home have altered things: reduced them, exposed their flaws somehow, and yet they are all tinged with fragments of familiarity which disconcert. He wonders why this territory, home ground after all, should seem so curiously alien.

A Saturday afternoon, the first warm weekend of the year. Dandelion parachutes skip in the breeze and gnats pirouette.

Pink horse-chestnut cones boat on viridian billows.

They meet knots of refugee men, brown men with sad eyes, lugging plastic carrier bags from Penny Saver, the cheapest supermarket in the city.

'It's like … different up here,' Laura says, staring around, 'well, a bit sort of dilapidated and forgotten.'

She's a Londoner, has never before penetrated much higher than Watford and is amazed by everything. 'Well and it's quaint, the accent is so weird, it's like another country.'

'Thanks a bunch,' he says and laughs, 'so I'm a curiosity as well, am I?' He tickles her ribs. Had they not been in the middle of a street, they would have rolled about giggling and whooping in one of their insane routines.

'Why exactly are you taking back those T-shirts your Mum bought you, Jamie?' she says, suddenly stern, switching topics as she often does.

'Because no way will I wear that jade green colour and sleeveless Ts. No chance.'

'But why not?' she persists.

'I am not that sort of person.'

'No?' She raises her eyebrows at him. 'What is that sort of person?'

'I am not a trendy and I am not a clubber, not that sort of clubber anyway, satisfied?'

'I don't get all this.'

'You wouldn't.'

'What does that mean?'

'Leave it.' He has a mind to go into a sulk but doesn't quite let himself. After all this is the first time he has brought Laura to meet his parents and it is in some way momentous, nerve-racking too. The awful bit would be if his Dad were to embarrass him, which he could easily do by making references to his babyhood, nappies etc. When they are alone together, they bandy insults, including 'dog-breath', 'wide-load', in a ritual which nobody else would be able to understand. The only problem is that his Dad can misjudge the occasion. Just thinking of his father makes Jamie smile. So far everything has been reasonably normal and not so eccentric as to make Laura comment.

The city centre vibrates with chart music from pub doorways and groups of men bellowing at one another. Bevies of girls prance by, legs flashing to the knicker-line and beyond, hair swooping in the breeze, stilettos rattling on pavements. The air carries washes of stale beer, body sprays, scents, fish and chips and fried onions from the burger stall. A *Big Issue* seller screeches his wares and a man with a scabby dog pipes 'Danny Boy' on a flute and now and then passers-by flip 20p coins into the margarine tub squatting before him.

They head for the shopping complex and the feel of her fingers shoots tendrils of electricity up his arm. He glances down at her green varnished toenails peeping from her wedge-heeled mules. She's wearing a tiny blue and green striped vest and stretch jeans that might be painted on. He has a strong urge to kiss her and nuzzle his face in her hair. He loves the smell of her hair, it hints at shampoo but something else warm and alive and resinous like pine trees in sunlight.

'That was once a dock,' he says, pointing to a bay of scummy water, which has a skin wrinkling on it like that on a mug of cold tea.

She stands for a moment staring down between the spiky railings.

'They've built this precinct partially over it. My Mum can remember seeing ships here.'

'Wow,' she says, 'it's quite mysterious really but well weird.'

They walk up a steep incline. Sun blasts through glass and beyond it the dock throws back the intense gleam. A stallholder presses silver-plated jewellery and watches at them. Opposite, teeny girls butterfly a store filled with hair ornaments: scrunchies, slides, mirrors, sparkly earrings, and combs, in fact all manner of candy-pink, baby-blue and silver delights for pre-teens and early teenagers.

She spots a store selling men's clothes. In the window models pose in chinos and striped polo shirts.

'Let's try in there,' she says. He knows this is not his type of shop at all, it's a clubber's paradise. In they go. He stares round, touches one or two T-shirts and shakes his head.

'What's wrong with these, they look fine to me?' she says.

'Not my scene.'

He heads out. They try a big department store next. Scarlet, cobalt, green, purple sleeveless T-shirts mass before them. T-shirts inscribed with all manner of logos dangle on rails. Batteries of polo shirts and short-sleeved cotton shirts flank the aisles.

'Plenty to choose from here,' she says, peering about and stroking some.

He's through them in a flash. 'Nah,' he says, 'no way.'

'I just don't get it,' she sighs with exasperation. 'I thought only women were as pernickety about clothes.'

'You don't understand.'

'No, I don't.'

'I've told you, clubbers wear this kind of gear. I'm not into that sort of style, well, clubbers of a certain sort and trendies. Anyway a lot of this is designer, CK and stuff.'

He feels irritated and frustrated by her persistence. Why the hell can't she understand? She knows his scene. She saw him mixing in the Union bar – funk, rap and jungle don't fit with trendies and chart music. They're a world apart. A cold heaviness lies on his chest. He shudders.

'What's wrong?' she says gazing at him, her eyes screwed up with curiosity.

'Nothing,' he says.

They visit several more shops, rattle the coat hangers in T.K. Maxx as they both sort through the rails. Nothing suitable.

Next come the sports shops. Some have gone over to designer gear, an absolute no-no.

'Better leave it for today,' he says. She is clearly fed up with the heat and the thrusting crowds.

'Look, we've come to get something, we can't stop now,' she says.

'It doesn't matter.'

'But it does, and you needn't snap.'

'I'm not.'

'Yes you are.'

'Not.' He pulls a face at her. She grimaces back.

'Bloody T-shirts,' she snarls, 'wish I'd never heard of them.'

'You can talk, what about when you're buying shoes?'

'That's not the same.' She flushes slightly.

They walk a couple of feet apart now. He's beginning to wish he had never asked her home to meet his parents. A gulf has cracked open between them. Until now they have never had a serious disagreement. He has a savage wish to end it all, tell her he can't carry on with the relationship as she doesn't understand him. This isn't what he has dreaded and he hates the unexpected.

'Let's have a drink,' she says, 'afternoon tea.'

Somehow that saves him. They find a café on the lower deck of the precinct, and whilst he's sitting opposite her, he falls again under the spell of her freckled nose and frizzy gingerish hair that spirals from her head in a mass of corkscrews, squiggles and satiny bits like a spaniel's ears. He wants to dig at her, tickle her, make her laugh, but decides it's too soon for a change in tone, and anyway she looks subdued. Perhaps the whole T-shirt thing has rattled her up. Perhaps now she's fed up with him, but he can't help it. He tells himself it is about identity; T-shirts are an outward sign of a person's identity.

She proffers the plate of Danish pastries. He remembers the silken surprise of her body last night as they lay in his old bedroom and is overcome with lust. She smiles but not too much, and he wants to put out a hand and seize her wrist and ask her if they're still friends, but he doesn't.

As the T-shirt shopping has become too dangerous, they abandon it by unspoken consent and he takes her on a wander round old streets, which once rang with clogs on cobbles and crates being loaded onto the quayside. Now the masts of yachts crowd the view and their rigging creaks in the breeze. Pink-faced men sit outside at tables over pints.

They saunter down to the pier from which the ferry used to chug forth and stand watching the estuary crinkling and froth-ing away to Lincolnshire. The air has a watery, smoky tang and plays on their faces, frizzling Laura's hair into a wild halo. He twines a question-mark curl round his finger but senses her drawing away from him. If only the day would stop swilling with undercurrents and stay steady.

In the early evening they start walking back. She says she's fine, prefers to walk rather than catch a bus. He observes her taking in the shabby little shops, the boarded-up places and the multiple takeaway outlets and the staggering drunks. She doesn't comment now but she continues to look and he's sure she's passing judgement.

'Fancy a drink before we land back on the wrinklies?' he asks.

'Mm, sounds good,' she says.

Under the influence of several Malibu and cokes Laura begins to smile, but Jamie still has the uncertain tension in his chest. He isn't sure where they are heading.

By the time he says he thinks they ought to be getting back because his mother will be expecting them for dinner, Laura seems quite relaxed.

All the while in the Duck and Drake, Jamie has been aware of a raucous group of sleeveless T-shirted townies flirting their muscles and their blue paisley-patterned arms. This group shove back their stools and make for the door at the same time as Jamie and Laura.

As Jamie reaches the door, he comes face to face with Wayne Sheldon, Wayne with his deceptively open face, retroussé nose and expressionless blue eyes. His arms bulge from the cutaway armholes of a white T-shirt. In that moment when their eyes meet, Jamie is back at school, hearing Wayne's tormentor's voice: Oh, poor little Jamie, what a pity he's lost his backpack.

Wayne and mates encircle him sniggering and jeering. They are the slow handclappers; the thugs who let his bike tyres down.

He's a head and shoulders taller than Wayne now. Wayne pretends he doesn't know Jamie and hustles out with his mates.

At that very moment three or four refugees happen to be passing the pub. Wayne yells, 'Kossies, whoa, Kossies, get 'em!' And he and his friends surround the refugees, who attempt to run for it, but don't succeed. The pub bouncers pelt out and Jamie rushes back into the pub and asks the barman to phone the police. 'Done it, mate,' the barman says, continuing to pull a pint, 'they'll ger here when it's all over.'

Laura waits at the door and her face is ashen.

By the time they go out into the street an ambulance and a police van are pulling away. Something stains the pavement, which looks like blood. Laura shivers.

A long time later when she's lying in bed with him, her head resting on his arm, he hears her say, 'I'm glad you didn't buy any sleeveless T-shirts.' His answer is a long slow kiss.